GW01159381

MONKEY BONES

By Rob Smales

Three Ravens Publishing
Chickamauga, GA USA

MONKEY BONES By Rob Smales
Published by Three Ravens Publishing
threeravenspublishing@gmail.com
P O Box 851, Chickamauga, GA 30707
https://www.threeravenspublishing.com
Copyright © 2024 by Rob Smales

All rights reserved. No part of this publication may be reproduced, distributed, or transmitted in any form or by any means, including photocopying, recording, or other electronic or mechanical methods, without the prior written permission of the publisher, except in the case of brief quotations embodied in critical reviews and certain other noncommercial uses permitted by copyright law.

For permission requests, contact the publisher listed above, addressed "Attention: Permissions".

Publishers Note: This is a work of fiction. Names, characters, places, and incidents are a product of the author's imagination. Locales and public names are sometimes used for atmospheric purposes. Any resemblance to actual people, living or dead, or to businesses, companies, events, institutions, or locales is completely coincidental.

Credits:
MONKEY BONES was written by Rob Smales
Cover design by: J.F. Posthumus
MONKEY BONES by: Rob Smales /Three Ravens Publishing – 1st edition, 2024

Ebook ISBN: 978-1-962791-88-5
Mass Market Paperback ISBN: 978-1-962791-89-2
Hardback ISBN: 978-1-962791-90-8

Table of Contents

Chapter 1

S ome people suggested it all started when he was hired, while others were more specific, claiming it began when he got his own route; Tom always said the shit started hitting the fan the day he met the cookie lady.

The day of the package.

The package was registered and heavy, far heavier than its size would suggest, and reminded Tom of another registered package he'd delivered a month earlier, on his first day with his new route: a package named Martin.

Martin, at least, had been clearly marked *Human Remains*; Tom hadn't needed to wait for the widow, signing for the package and telling him who—and thus what—was inside, to know what was going on. Tom had wanted to deliver Martin first, rather than waiting until the middle of his route, when he usually got to the house where Martin had lived. It had felt creepy, and the delivery would be awkward, and he'd just wanted to get rid of his cremated copilot ASAP.

"The general public thinks the postal service is boring," said his supervisor, Paul, when Tom had asked about deviating to deliver Martin. Tom was the youngest carrier in the office, and Paul enjoyed *handing down wisdom* in his own, irreverent manner. "And sometimes it is. But that's just the down time between the really fucking weird times. Like when a naked old person opens the door to take the mail from you, or when a guy with no legs accuses you of stealing his shoe catalog, or—" He'd aimed a finger gun at Tom and dropped the hammer. "—when you have to deliver a cremated body. Welcome to the wonderful world of weird, my friend." Then he'd walked away.

Tom had taken this as permission and delivered Martin first.

With this new package, however, he had no such luck.

The post office workfloor was warehouse like—big, square, and open, with a thirty-foot ceiling—with carrier sorting benches set around the perimeter and the supervisor's desk in the center, but even in this big space, Paul's voice seemed a trifle overloud as he shook his head. "Doesn't say *human remains* on there that I can see."

"Well, no." Tom tapped the shoebox-sized brown-paper-wrapped box on his bench. "But we can't tell *what* it says, can we? Unless you can read Russian, I mean?"

The parcel bore more international post stamps than Tom thought there were countries, and the shipping label had been filled out almost entirely in the Cyrillic alphabet. The only things in English were the name and address of the intended. But still, just as with Martin, the creep factor felt high.

Paul snorted a laugh. "No, I can't. And neither can you."

"But it's heavy. *Really* heavy."

"But it doesn't say *human remains*." Paul tapped the mostly illegible label. "That shit there might say *fourteen-inch solid rubber dildo as thick as your wrist* for all we know. Those fuckers are heavier than you'd think."

Tom felt his face try to make three different expressions at once. "What? I don't ... Wait, how do you—"

"Never you mind. Look, kid, you're the last one out of the office this morning. Just deliver it when you get to the house."

"But I'm telling you, it feels just like that urn full of dude." Tom poked the package. "Go on, heft it."

Paul grinned, showing his palms in a *hands-off* gesture. "Hey, you heft your own wrist-thick fourteen-inch solid rubber dildo. That shit is *not* my job!"

"Could you keep it down?" Face growing hot, knowing he was blushing, and Paul was enjoying every second of it, Tom glanced around to see if anyone was listening. "Someone's gonna really think—"

But when he looked back, Paul was gone. Baffled, Tom scanned the area again; he'd only looked away for a second, and the nearest place the supervisor might have ducked into was more than twenty feet away.

"How does he *do* that?"

No one was there to answer his question, nor advise him on the cremains. Or dildo. Or whatever. Sighing, Tom scooped the box off his bench to bring it out to his truck.

Chapter 2

Standing in the hall before the door to eighty-two Fernald Court, surprisingly heavy box under his arm, Tom sighed again.

Fernald Court was old age housing, a horseshoe-shaped private way with a pair of big cul-de-sacs on the outside of the curve—almost a Fernald Court East and a Fernald Court West, with some units out on the horseshoe itself, as if the cul-de-sacs were putting out shoots—lined with squat-looking cubes of sand-colored brick. Some of the east and west buildings backed right onto each other, and a series of interconnected walkways made it easier for the old folks to get along the entire court, the whole thing putting Tom in mind of an industrialized Hobbiton, designed by someone with an eye toward functionality rather than imagination.

Each building was comprised of four units: basement, first floor, second floor, third. He'd been focused that morning on what might be *in* the box, rather than where it was going, or to whom. He'd only been the regular carrier on this route for a month and hadn't met all four hundred of his customers yet. Apparently, eighty-two Fernald Court was the basement unit in the east side where he'd find one Anna Preobrazhenskaya, and, thanks to Paul, he desperately hoped he held the cremated remains of a human being tucked tight to his armpit.

If it turned out he was delivering some seventy-five-year-old Russian widow's wrist-thick, fourteen-inch solid rubber dildo, he might never recover. For Christ's sake, his *nana* was seventy-five!

Does that mean she—

Suppressing a shudder, he poked the doorbell, wincing at the shrill buzzer—then gave a little *"Yip!"* when the door snapped open like a jack-in-the-box lid. Also like a jack-in-the-box, the apartment's occupant popped out onto the welcome mat right in front of him, and only the fact that he'd just expelled his breath in the *yip* kept him from screaming.

The woman's face was melting.

No, not melting, Tom saw an instant later. Coated. With some kind of ... goop. Like one of those mud masks his mom wore, but this was clear, and thick, and ... Vaseline? Goose grease? Tallow rendered from the corpses of children? Tom had a vivid imagination, and it was starting to run away with him here. He was still considering the scream when the gelatin mask split and a wide mouth opened.

"Can I hilp you?"

Tom blinked. "Excuse me?"

A sticklike arm rose, twiglike finger indicating the doorbell. "You rrring bill. Can I hilp you?" The mouth turned up at the corners in what *might* have been a pleasant smile. Hard to tell under all that ... whatever.

That rolling R ... I ring—Oh! Bell! *"Can I* help *you?"* Tom gave himself a mental facepalm. *You're surprised the old Russian widow has a Russian accent? Duh?*

Now that he knew her flesh was merely slick, not sloughing, he managed to take in the rest of her. His sticklike/twiglike impression bore through. Those thin arms stuck out of a thick stump body that might have been five feet tall if she stood *very* straight, sheathed in a bright yellow housecoat—and nothing else, if the vertical drop of some truly prodigious boobs was any indication. The legs thrusting out from under that screaming yellow wrap were as thin and sticklike as the arms, ending in bare feet so gnarled and bent with bunions and bones they looked more like roots than toes. They also would have looked too big on Tom himself, though he towered over the little lady by nearly a foot. The overall effect, especially when he spotted her matching yellow head scarf capping a mass of hair curlers, was ...

Wow, he thought. *Just ... wow.*

The pleasant smile waited.

"Sorry! Yes, I rang your bill. Bell. Yes. I—uh, I have a registered package for ..." He squinted, but even with the familiar alphabet, the name scrawled in a large, looping hand gave him trouble. "Mrs., uh, Preo ... Preobraz ..."

"*Pree-oh-brajin-sky-ah*," she enunciated, and he got the feeling she'd been through this before. "Is me. I need to sign?"

"Yes, please." He held out the package, slip and pen on top, offering it as a writing surface, but she merely plucked the box from his hands.

"Careful! That's heavy!"

"Oh, I know is heavy." She stepped back inside to place the box on a small doorside table. "Is burial urn. Clay. Very thick."

"Burial urn?" *Son of a bitch, it* is *a body!*

She looked back over a shoulder, and he heard the smile in her voice. "Oh, no you worry. Is not *full*! Is antique."

"Oh!" Tom was kind of impressed. "You ordered an antique urn all the way from ... uh ..." He pointed toward the return address. "Wherever that is?"

She picked up the pen and signature slip. "*That* is—" She made a series of sounds like a garbage disposal working on a particularly thick bone, a Russian word Tom had no hope of understanding or reproducing; he couldn't even identify any vowels in there. "And I not order. I have on-call there who owns shop. He send me thing I might find interesting."

On-call? Uncle? She has an uncle? He saw no wrinkles through the goop, but her hands and feet looked so old and dry they'd probably make good kindling. *If she has an uncle who's still alive, the man must get birthday cards from God.*

"That's still cool." He pointed to the slip in her hand. "If you could just sign on the—"

"You are new mealman?"

"New ... ? I'm your new regular, yes. My name's Tom."

"Hold on. I have something for you."

"Oh, all I really need is your sig—" But it was no use. The shiny tiny tank of a woman turned and trundled away, each throw-pillow-sized buttock seeming to move independently, yet both working together to eat the back of that housecoat. He watched, horrifically fascinated, as the chewing cheeks made their way across the room and through an open doorway, disappearing deeper into the apartment. He gave himself a light shake and, making sure not to actually cross the threshold (he hadn't been invited) peered curiously at what he could see of her place.

The front door opened to the living room, with a box arch into the kitchen beyond it and a hallway back there on the left, connecting the living room with ... wherever the old woman had disappeared to.

An Afghan-covered loveseat sat on the edge of an area rug with its matching easy chair, facing the huge TV beside the front door—no flatscreen or smart TV, but a monstrous tubed dinosaur probably weighing as much as Tom himself. And as old as those things appeared, everything else looked far older.

Rather than a shade of cloth or paper, the lamp beside the loveseat was all of cut crystal, and he wasn't certain it used electricity. The end table it sat upon had three drawers, four legs, and more fretwork than your average gingerbread house. He'd no idea what wood it was carved from—and that was the impression it somehow gave, that it had been carved by hand rather than cut by machine—but it was a deep reddish brown, and he didn't think you'd find a rich sheen like that in an Ikea catalog.

The coffee table seemed to be of the same wood, and though the fretwork wasn't exactly the same, they still seemed to match. Different set, same maker, maybe? It was covered with smaller things, all of them radiating a sense of money and age: a trio of small stone elephants walking in a line, tusks carved from what appeared to be real ivory and eyes of different, more precious stone; a glass perfume bottle with a squeeze bulb on the end of a rubber tube, he thought it was called an *atomizer*?; a polished skull that startled him for a moment, thinking it was a child—it was about the size of a man's fist—until he saw the fanged dentition in the elongated jaw and knew it for some kind of monkey. It still would have been exceptionally creepy if not for the incongruously modern TV remote balanced atop the shiny dome.

Even amidst this exhibition of old things, there were some modern conveniences you just didn't go without.

There was more, but before he could register everything, Mrs. Preobrazhenskaya came bustling back.

"Here you are."

She handed him his pen, the signed slip, and a pack of Goya chocolate cookies: twenty cocoa wafers in a golden foil-paper tube.

"There. Now you have snek."

It was on the tip of his tongue to refuse, to say *No thank you* and *Really, that's not necessary* and *Oh, I'm still full from lunch.* More experienced carriers had warned him about accepting food from the old folks. Old eyes sometimes have difficulty reading the lines on the measuring cup, they'd said, or keeping their teaspoons and tablespoons straight, or even, occasionally, sugar and salt. And that's to say nothing of telling whether those measuring cups and spoons were actually *clean.*

But this was an unopened, store-bought package of cookies, and she'd made a special trip into the bowels of her home to fetch them for him, and ... and besides, beneath that grease slick covering her features, he thought she looked really pleased to be giving them to him.

He tucked the pen and slip into his shirt pocket, smiled and gave her a little salute with the Goyas.

"Thank you, Mrs. Preob ... ah, Mrs. P."

Beneath the grease, Mrs. P. beamed.

And that was how Tom met the cookie lady.

Chapter 3

He learned how to pronounce Preobrazhenskaya, but did so only rarely. To her face he called her *Mrs. P.*, while in his head and when discussing her at home and in the office, she remained *the cookie lady*, because at least once a week he rang her bell with a registered package (he never even came *close* to pronouncing either the uncle's name or his town), and every time, she stomped off into the depths of her apartment, holding the pen and slip hostage until he accepted his package of Goyas.

The seasons passed, and Tom met nearly all of his four hundred customers—a few people were just never home—a hundred of whom lived in the sprawl that was Fernald Court, known to some of the older letter carriers as *Wrinkle City*. Wrinkle City, populated entirely by retirees, was where he actually saw his customers most frequently: folks in ground-floor units waved from their windows as he went by; men and women, lined up like ancient schoolchildren waiting patiently for their turn to climb shakily up into the GLS seniors bus, called out *hello*s and *how are ya*s when he pulled up; and concerned grandmothers (never grandfathers, he noticed, and what was up with that?) met him by their mailboxes to ask if the oversized, festively-colored envelopes they handed him would be delivered before their grandson or granddaughter's birthday next week.

In short, he got to know his peeps.

In the summer, he helped several residents refill their water coolers, those five gallon bottles being a bit much for septuagenarians to handle.

In the fall, Mrs. Gerritson, a tiny woman with a James Earl Jones voice that spoke to decades of cigarettes, asked him to pour her a glass of wine.

"The grocer dropped that off on Saturday," she intoned, pointing an obviously arthritic finger to a gallon jug sitting on the counter. "I've been trying for two days, but I can't lift that thing to pour. Would you mind?"

He poured, then asked if she'd ever looked into boxed wine. "Once it's on the counter, you just use the built-in spigot. No heavy lifting."

A week later, Mrs. Gerritson tapped the window as he passed, toasting him with a glass of wine—drawn, he assumed, from the box of Vella on the counter.

In the winter, Tom received Christmas cards from all the old folks—one fellow, Mr. Barry, somehow mailing it directly to Tom's apartment, "To make sure *you're* the one who gets it."

Being tracked down like that had freaked Tom out a little, but it turned out Mr. Barry had ferreted out facts for *The Boston Globe* for nearly forty years.

"Sure, I'm nosey," the old man said. "But I'm *professionally* nosey. Or, I was. And after four decades, that's a hard habit to break, kid."

The retired reporter put paid to any theories about gossip being something only old *women* engaged in. Mr. Barry lived in a ground floor apartment, and Tom discovered he merely had to unlock the mailbox for the old man to open the door to unit eighty-five and start spouting what Tom thought of as *The Wrinkle City News*. The ex-newsman still knew how to tell a story, and by talking to him, Tom was able to keep up with all the goings-on, even of the folks he didn't see regularly.

And right around once a week—skipping a week occasionally, but sometimes doubling up—Mrs. P. would get a package from Uncle Unpronounceable, and Tom would get his Goyas. He figured she bought the damned things by the case, and as time passed they worked their way through the cocoas and into sugar cookies. He watched the stuff in her living room change: the trio of elephants replaced by a cut glass candy dish, for example, and the atomizer swapped out for a small fancy set of binoculars (Google told him these were opera glasses, which he took to mean *small fancy binoculars*).

He learned Mrs. P. had two faces: the indoor, *I'm old enough not to give a fuck and I want to be comfortable* face, and her outside, public face. In public, the cookie lady was always dressed to impress, in well-fitted dresses over some marvel of undergarment engineering that heaved and held her geographic bust into something resembling the prow of an icebreaker, putting a yard of horizontal cleavage beneath her chin. Her makeup was perfect, and though she was eighty if she was a day, her face was smooth as a baby's bare ass, neither smile lines nor crow's feet making an appearance; either she had Hollywood-level skills with the powder and brush, or that grease she wore on her at-home face was just about magical, and her auburn locks held not a hint of gray.

What impressed him most about her outside face was her shoes: always shiny, always fashionable, and always *small.* The overall transformation was impressive, but those shoes were actually startling. At home and barefoot, her feet were big and broad, and if he hadn't seen her wearing such small, pointed shoes with his own eyes, Tom would have claimed it an impossibility.

He *still* thought it impossible those shoes could be *comfortable*. Whenever he saw the cookie lady out and about, he always marveled anew. *Just wedging her feet in there has to hurt,* he thought, *never mind actually* walking *in them!* But she showed no hint of discomfort, just smiled and chatted, as friendly and pleasant as if she'd worn big, comfy house slippers, or was as barefoot as she always chose to be at home. Over time, Tom came to the conclusion that the little lady just thought certain things, like her outside face, should be a certain way, and would go to great lengths to make that happen. That she'd smile through such discomfort and spend all her at-home time wearing a grease mask in constant preparation for her outside face showed a kind of old world iron will, he thought. He actually found it kind of impressive, and a little endearing.

Looking back on it later, he found it a touch frightening as well.

Chapter 4

It was spring, warm and sunny, just the kind of afternoon that encouraged people to call out to him, *Wish I had your job*. Tom had been doing the route for so long by then, he tended to walk around on a kind of autopilot. With a bounce in his step, humming "Despacito"—the whole song was in Spanish, and he didn't understand a word, but it was still catchy as hell—he opened the door to the cookie lady's building and strode inside. He registered Mrs. P. and Mrs. Nelson standing down by the cookie lady's door with a "Good afternoon, ladies," as he unlocked the top of the four-unit mailbox set in the ground-floor wall. He'd opened the box and was actually shoving in the first bit of mail before he realized he'd walked in on an argument.

"I'll just clean it up." Tom was startled by Mrs. Nelson's volume. "Honestly, it's no big deal."

"*No* just clean up," the cookie lady thundered—actually *thundered*. "Is fourth time happen! Is fourth time *this month*!"

"Well I'm *sorry*!" Mrs. Nelson didn't sound sorry at all. "She knows she shouldn't be out of the apartment. She's not an outside cat. I'm just glad when she *does* get out, she stays here in the hall instead of going out and getting lost, or hit by a car or something."

Tom knew what they were talking about then: at least a couple of times a month, he himself opened the door to find a fluffy white cat in this very hall. Seeing it always filled him with a slight panic, afraid the creature would escape and it would be viewed as his fault. The cat—it wore a tagged collar, but he'd never gotten close enough to actually read the thing—hadn't made a break for it yet, but Tom was very aware that it *could*.

"You no can take care of *ket*, you no should *have* ket."

The mailbox key was on a belt chain, and with it stuck in the open box, Tom was effectively chained to the wall, but when he leaned back enough he could peek around the second floor stairs and down toward the basement. He couldn't see the cookie lady, but could make out Mrs. Nelson's back as she stood on the bottom step. Amelia Nelson had been a lawyer in her earlier life, and so far as Tom could figure, she hadn't lost either her ability to persuade or delegate when she'd left the bar. As tall as Tom, with a body toned whip-thin from tennis and sailing (two of her many man-friends had boats, according to Mr. Barry) and kept nut-brown year round by sun and sunlamp, Mrs. Nelson (again, according to *The Wrinkle City News*) chaired three boards around town, helped run the local animal shelter, and was in the process of getting a sort of residents' association together there at Fernald Court. Usually, when Tom saw her, she was either telling someone what to do or taking them to task for doing it wrong; the groundskeeping staff lived in fear of her.

Now, however, this woman for whom the phrase *take charge* had seemingly been invented, took an unsteady step back, stumbling up to tower two stairs over her shorter opponent. "I'm allowed a pet. It's in the lease. One small pet." The words were sure, but her voice wasn't.

The cookie lady, on the other hand, sounded absolutely sure of herself. "No take care of *ket*, no should *have* ket. No *will* have ket!"

Mrs. Nelson backed another step toward Tom. "I *can* have a cat! It's in the lease, you stupid woman! In the lease!"

"*Can.*" The cookie lady's voice was loud, deep, and guttural. "But *won't.*"

Mrs. Nelson, one-time courtroom powerhouse, current runner of committees, and terror of the maintenance crew, turned on her heel and pounded up the stairs, and though she cupped her lower face with one hand, the eyes above that hand were tear shiny. Overhearing the argument had filled Tom with that same awkward feeling he'd had the few times he'd been present while his parents were fighting, and the wish to be just about anywhere else in the world. Despite that, he tried to ask if Mrs. Nelson was all right, but she brushed past him on her way to her third floor unit, and the door up there slammed.

Still just wanting to be out of there, Tom shoved mail into the boxes with all speed, locked the top panel back up, and headed for the door. As he turned from the mailboxes, the basement stairs came into view again—and so did the cookie lady, standing on the top step.

Tom hadn't heard her go into her own apartment, but had assumed—hoped?—he'd just missed it under the noise of Mrs. Nelson hustling up the stairs. The squat vision in yellow, so close, motionless and silent as death, startled him. "Oh! Good afternoon, Mrs. P."

The cookie lady never looked at him—didn't even know he was there, as far as he could tell—but stared fixedly upward, as if somehow still watching Amelia Nelson, and her face, what he could make out of it through its shiny coating, was hard as a stone. He waited an uncomfortable beat.

"Well, uh, have a nice day." He stepped toward the door. "But *won't.*"

Tom paused, half afraid he was about to hear a litany of complaints against the other woman. But the cookie lady had already turned and started down the stairs, muttering to herself in no language Tom understood. She lifted her knees and stomped her feet flat like a wind-up toy, except when she stepped carefully into her apartment over the welcome mat, the exact center of which held a single, prodigious cat turd.

Chapter 5

The following Monday, flyers appeared on every front
door along Fernald Court.
LOST: FLUFFY
IF FOUND, PLEASE CALL
555-1372

P rofessionally printed and laminated for protection
from sun and weather, the photo was a grainy shot
of a cat in profile, an obvious blow-up from
another photo. Still, even through the pixelization and
poor angle, Tom recognized the animal: Mrs. Nelson's
welcome-mat-shitting escapee.

I guess she finally made a break for it, he thought. *I feel bad for
Mrs. Nelson, but ...* He remembered a crew of a half-dozen
men, all standing at a ragged sort of attention and looking
uncomfortable as the tall tanned woman harangued them
about how they were mulching the shrubbery, and gave
himself a little shake. *I'm just glad it wasn't me.*

When he brought Mrs. P. her delivery from Uncle
Unpronounceable that day, the cookie lady was her usual,
pleasant self. She had a brand new welcome mat beneath
her gnarled toes, and they must have gone through her
whole stock of sugar cookies, because she started giving
him cocoa again that day.

Three days later, all the flyers were gone.

"The HVAC guys found it, while they were here checking all the vents and stuff," said Mr. Barry, small and wiry but for a growing retiree's paunch, leaning in his doorjamb while Tom filled the mailboxes.

"So she got Fluffy back?"

"Oh, no." The old man tugged the bill of his fishing hat. "They found the collar, lying up there on the roof under some ductwork or something. That and the, uh, the tail."

Tom stared. "They found Fluffy's *tail*?"

"Yup. Said there was some fur, and, you know, some other mess. Guy told me he would have thought a hawk got a squirrel, you know, the way they do—and I don't know if you know, but we've had hawks nesting on our roofs before. Makes a mess of the heating vents and stuff. No nest up there now. Same crew removed one last year from just down the street, though, and he wasn't going to look too closely at that tail until he saw the collar. 'Squirrel might have a fluffy tail,' guy said, 'but I ain't never seen one with an ID tag.'"

Of course the old newshound had even gotten a quote from the guy who found it—even got a quote. And hawks nesting on roofs? Every summer, Tom had some little winged passerby—Thrushes? Sparrows? Tom wasn't up on his ornithology—decide the open sill ledge beside his window-mounted air conditioner was the perfect place to build a nest, protected from the elements by the building, the window, and the air conditioner itself. They packed their shit in, happily weaving their little homes, completely oblivious to the fact that a big ugly human lived just to the other side of that thin plastic accordion slider they were scratching against with twigs, straw, and their own little toes. He always showed himself, frightened them into moving on, but those were just *little* birds. He had literally *no idea* how he'd handle it if his sill-squatter were ever big and fierce enough to take out a cat and strip it down to just a collar and tail.

"Jesus."

Mr. Barry nodded. "Yeah. Amelia's already squawking about exterminators, demanding to be in charge of the process, you know, the way she does."

Tom locked the box and handed the old man his mail. "Exterminators?"

"Oh, sure." Mr. Barry straightened to go back into his apartment. "No hawk nests up there *now*, so maybe it was rats—and if the rats have started taking down the cats, that's a bad sign, dontcha think?"

"I guess so," Tom said, though in his mind he heard a deep voice muttering two threat-packed words: *But won't*.

Rob Smales

Chapter 6

Through the rest of the spring, Tom noticed a change around Fernald Court. There had always been residents hanging around outside, no matter the season, and in all weather but pouring rain. Their apartments weren't the most spacious digs in the world, and quite a few of the old folks took advantage of the benches and ice cream tables scattered about their courtyards, gathering to talk, or play checkers and chess, or just sitting out where they could watch the world go by. Mrs. Gerritson, whom Tom suspected was the oldest citizen of Wrinkle City—he wasn't about to ask, but from the look of her, in her younger days the wizened creature just may have babysat little Georgie Washington—had once told Tom that daily fresh air was the secret to a long and happy life. She'd then pulled on her unfiltered cigarette so long and deep she seemed to take the smoke in all the way to her toes.

Tom suspected her secret was really tar, permeating her entire body from the inside and preserving her like those bog bodies he kept reading about; mummification by American Spirit.

As weeks went by and the days grew warmer, however, though people still paired up to play chess and Parcheesi, the discussion groups changed. They were still gathering, but more often than not, only one person was doing the talking.

Amelia Nelson.

One day, the GLS bus dropped Mr. Barry off while Tom was in his front hall, already chained to the mailboxes and working.

"Hi, Tom." The old reporter, paper grocery bag tucked to his chest with one arm, jingled his keyring as he approached, frowning, trying to separate out his door key one-handed.

"She trying to organize an uprising or something?"

Mr. Barry looked up. "Huh?"

Tom jerked his chin toward the narrow window beside the outer door, through which he could see Mrs. Nelson holding forth to a half dozen people.

Mr. Barry turned, followed Tom's line of sight, and grunted.

"Oh. Uh, that's probably about Anna Preo-bresh-whatsis. Her downstairs neighbor."

"Preobrazhenskaya," Tom said.

"Yeah. Her." He'd found the right key and reached for the door.

"What about her?"

"The cat," the old man said over his shoulder. The hall was filled with the sudden rasp of a key violating a lock, but Tom's head was filled with the memory of arguing voices and a teary-eyed Amelia Nelson. He waited for the old man to go on, but was surprised to hear the door open instead. He looked up to see Mr. Barry step across the threshold and pause, bracing the door with a foot to work the key back out of the lock.

"Wait! What about the cat?"

Mr. Barry half turned to him, conflict clearly stamped across his features: the need to put his groceries away warring with an old gossip's desire to shoot the shit.

"Amelia says it's Anna's fault, what happened. None of us see how it *could* be, but she's pretty damned insistent. Seems awfully far-fetched to me, though. *Awfully* far-fetched."

You didn't hear them arguing, Tom thought. *Or the tone of Mrs. P.'s voice.* It was on the tip of his tongue to tell Mr. Barry that it didn't seem all that far-fetched to him—that, in fact, he'd already considered the possibility. In the wake of overhearing them arguing about that very cat, how could he not? And though he couldn't envision the ungainly woman actually *catching* the animal—oh, maybe if it was asleep and had at least one leg in a trap—his vivid imagination came up with a saucer of drugged or poisoned milk easily enough. Physically, it was possible, and she had what the TV cop dramas called *motivation.* But the thing he kept coming up against, whenever he thought about it, was the roof. She might want to hide the body, sure, but getting it up on the roof? How? The maintenance guys used thirty-foot ladders, and he was pretty sure Mrs. P. didn't have one of those stashed somewhere. Had she thrown it? He couldn't picture the cookie lady, all done up in her outside face, hair and makeup perfect and tottering about on those little high-heeled shoes, swinging a dead cat around hard enough to fling it onto a third-story roof. Besides, hadn't Mr. Barry said they'd found what was left of Fluffy under a duct up there?

But a cat, climbing up onto a roof? A cat curious enough to escape Mrs. Nelson's unit so often it had become a regular thing? Sure, he could see that. And anywhere cats could go, rats could go too, he was sure. And what about a hawk? Hadn't the HVAC guy said it looked like a hawk had gotten a squirrel? Tom spent enough time outside every day to have seen a few of them. Or maybe it was the same one. Who knew? But they were up there sometimes, soaring around. And an indoor cat, not versed in the dangers of the outside world, having achieved the roof and checking it out, unaware of death from above on stooping wings ... Yeah, he could see it.

So maybe a cat-killing cookie lady wasn't as far-fetched as Mr. Barry thought, but there were other, more logical scenarios. And so, yes, it was on the tip of Tom's tongue to tell Mr. Barry about the argument, maybe explain a little of Amelia Nelson's thinking, but he didn't. Telling the gossipy Mr. Barry, he knew, was tantamount to telling *everyone*, and there was no way the cookie lady wouldn't hear that Tom had seriously considered her in some bizarre cat-assassin scenario. He rang her bell at least once a week, and that would make the awkwardness of that old Martin delivery pale in comparison.

So he merely nodded to Mr. Barry and said, "Sounds far-fetched to me."

The old guy smiled faintly and held up his grocery bag as if for inspection. "If you'll excuse me, I've got to, uh ..."

But as Mr. Barry disappeared into his apartment, Tom's mind's ear heard two words again, echoing slightly in the empty hallway, heavy with menace and, it turned out, prophetic.

But won't.

Chapter 7

It was early summer when Mrs. Nelson decided it was time to talk to Tom. He'd just collected a signature from the cookie lady, dropping off yet another package from Uncle Unpronounceable, and was leaving the building, Goya packet in hand. The sun was warm and the groundskeeping crew had been by earlier, leaving the air filled with the scent of fresh-cut grass. As the door swung shut behind him, he heard a harsh "*Pssst!*" He looked left, then right—and was just in time to catch Mrs. Nelson peeking around the corner of her building, cupping a hand to her face to focus the sound again.

"*Pssst!*"

Tom had seen the lip-popping, teeth-hissing, attention-getting sound represented in books, but in a lifetime of television and movies, not to mention interacting with people in the real world, he'd never heard of anyone actually *using* it. He raised his eyebrows, pointing to his own chest in the classic *Who, me?* and received an exasperated beckon and nod.

Tom's heart fell. If Mrs. Nelson wanted to talk to him, she'd likely be expressing her dissatisfaction about something—in Tom's experience, Mrs. Nelson never *complained*, she *expressed dissatisfaction*, often until her target was in tears—though if she wanted to do it in private, he felt he was in luck. This was the same woman who'd dressed the entire groundskeeping staff down out in the street. Twice. That he knew of. He started over.

"Can I help you, Mrs.—"

"*Shhh!*" She waved a frantic hand, then reversed the motion into another beckon, *sotto voce* mouthing the words *Just come here.*

Heart falling further, he rounded the corner; he still smelled the grass, but the temperature dipped as he stepped into the building's shadow. Once he'd passed, she leaned over to peer back the way he'd come, as if checking for anyone tailing him. This was really strange. The fashionable sweatsuit was right, as was the tight cap of white curls, and according to the somewhat sun-leathered face, this was Amelia Nelson. But the Mrs. Nelson Tom (and, he was pretty sure, everyone else) knew and feared never minded being the center of attention—often demanded it, in fact. *This* Mrs. Nelson was hiding, checking his back trail, and even now turned to him with wide eyes and a stage whisper.

"I need to talk to you, and she can't know, all right?"

"Who?" Tom said, sure he already knew.

"Anna. I need to talk to you about Anna Preobrazhenskaya, and I don't want her to hear. Or know. Do you understand?"

That last question had a bit of steel in it, a little of the old Mrs. Nelson, and though he thought she'd meant it as something of a threat, he found it strangely comforting. He nodded and shrugged. "Yeah, sure. What can I—"

"What can you tell me about those packages she gets?"

Tom blinked. "Well ... nothing, really. I mean, I don't think I'm supposed to tell you about anyone else's mail. It's an ethics thing. But honestly, just that gets them, that's really all I could tell you anyway."

Her eyes grew hard, her voice intense, though she kept it low. "What's in them?"

He shrugged. "I don't know. I just deliver 'em. She says they're antiques. Why? What's this about?"

"Fluff—uh, my ca ... I ..." She sighed. "Look, I know you know about my cat. Everybody knows, I think. But you ... you were there. You heard her threaten me. You ... I ..."

He figured he understood her difficulty: he'd been there when this proud woman had run upstairs, cowed into tears by her downstairs neighbor. She probably didn't like thinking about it, couldn't possibly like talking about it, but here she was, trying to discuss it with the lone witness to what she likely considered her disgrace.

Tom was uncomfortable, seeing her in such distress, neighborhood hard-ass or not. He nodded, trying to help her over the hump. "I heard her, yeah."

Her gaze sharpened. "So you know."

It was a statement, not a question, and though part of Tom just wanted to agree and be on his way, the equivocation popped out. "Know what?"

She gave an eye roll to the side and a limp shrug, universal sign language for *Oh God, how dense can you be?*

"You know she killed Fluffy!"

His mind flashed back to his conversation with Mr. Barry. "Hey, no! I mean, I don't think it's as far-fetched as some people are making out, but—"

Mrs. Nelson leaned forward, eyes bright and hard in her tanned face, a hawk stooping on an unsuspecting house pet. "But you heard her!"

Tom nodded. "I heard her, yeah. But the *roof*? I—" He spread his hands. "How?"

She settled back, the killing stoop aborted. "Yeah. I keep running into that. *That's* the part I can't figure."

"So, I'm sorry, but ..."

He took a step to leave, but her eyes went hard once more. "You were there for the threat, but you weren't there after. After Fluffy was ... found. People around here who'd heard about it—and that's *everybody*, thanks to Will—were offering condolences. Everyone. It's what you *do* in a community like this. Even people who don't particularly like pets, like Mr. and Mrs. Bobski, were nice to me about it. But not that bitch downstairs."

She scrunched, drawing her head and shoulders down, flexed her cheeks to stretch her lips comically wide, and pulled a sneer. Just as Tom figured out what she was doing, the ex-lawyer broke into an accent so thick, in Bullwinkle terms, it would have been Natasha times Boris.

"So *soo-ry* to hear 'bout yoor *ket*, so bed 'bout *ket*, but I till, I till you! You no should hev *ket*. I till, I till, bat you no lee-sen! Poor, poor *ket*. If on-lee you lee-sen. Poor, poor *ket*. You should hev lee-sen to me."

Straightening, she dropped the accent. "She stood there, spouting that *you should have listened to me* bullshit and grinning through that collagen crap she wears all the time. She was gloating. Gloating! Like some mafia collection man coming around to the little shop owner who wouldn't pay, after his business has burned to the ground, saying *Oh, hey, too bad about that fire! Bet you wish now you'd paid for our insurance, yeah? I always said this place was an accident waiting to happen* ... She did it. She practically *said* she did it. But I ... yeah, I can't figure out that roof thing."

"Me either," said Tom. "And I did think about it, back when it happened. But—"

"But that's not what I wanted to talk to you about."

"Excuse me?"

Mrs. Nelson shook her head, not in negation, it seemed, but more in an attempt to clear it. "I'm—I'm sorry. I got off on a tangent, but I really got you over here to ask about her packages."

"Okay." Tom's eyes narrowed. "But I've told you all I—"

"See, I can't figure out the roof thing, but I know she did Fluffy. So I've been investigating her."

"You—"

"I still know people, and I know how investigating's done. I've been out of the game awhile, but I haven't lost all my chops. I can still check records and backtrack people with the best of them. You know what I found out about Anna Preobrazhenskaya?"

Tom shrugged.

"Nothing. Not a thing. It's like before she came to live here, Anna Preobrazhenskaya didn't exist."

The plots from a dozen movies danced through his head. "Witness protection?"

He thought she'd laugh, but Amelia Nelson merely raised her eyebrows and nodded. "Not bad. That was my first thought, too. Except in my digging and backtracking, the earliest record I can find is her application for residence at eighty-two Fernald Court. Know when she filled it out?"

He shrugged again.

"Nineteen eighty-six."

He started to shrug a third time, but froze, calculating furiously. "But that's ... what, thirty years?"

"Thirty-three. Want to know her stated age at the time of application?"

"Uh ..."

"Seventy-six."

Tom's mouth moved for a second without sound, his brain whirling. "But that'd make her ... a hundred and nine?"

"A hundred and nine," Mrs. Nelson echoed. "I might have to start smearing some of that chicken fat on *my* face. But even all this isn't what I wanted to talk to you about."

He tried to focus, not *dazed* exactly, but maybe overwhelmed. If this was all real, it was, well ... Like Paul had said, back when he'd gotten the route, *Welcome to the wonderful world of weird.* But as far as what she wanted to talk to him about—

"Her packages."

Mrs. Nelson nodded. "Her packages. Full of antiques, she says?"

"Uh-huh."

"And she gets about one a week?"

"Sounds about right."

"Sounds about right to me, too. I've been her upstairs neighbor for five years, but Candice, on the second floor, she's been there for eight. She says those packages have been arriving about once a week the whole time she's been here. Some of them are pretty big, aren't they?"

Tom puffed air in thought. "Well, I guess maybe half of them are too big to fit in my satchel, so I have to make a special trip for them. Those can get kind of big, yeah."

"So. One a week would be fifty-two a year, but let's make the math a little easier and round it to fifty. Fifty antiques a year, over just the eight years we know about, that makes four hundred items, at least half of them big enough to require their own trips in for delivery. *Four hundred.*" She raised her eyebrows at him. "Where are they?"

Tom made a face to go along with this shrug. "I don't know. Her place?"

"I know what her apartment is like. It's the same size as mine—these units all have the same basic floor plan. Never mind two hundred things that qualify as *big*, if I tried to store four hundred pairs of *shoes* in my place, they'd be coming out my ass."

Tom held up a hand. "But there's nothing saying she's *kept* all the stuff she gets. Maybe she's sold stuff, or even given it away. Maybe she has a storage unit somewhere."

Mrs. Nelson was already shaking her head. "She doesn't bring anything anywhere. She doesn't have a car—has never had a license, as far as I can find out, and that's something I *should* be able to find—and almost no one rides the fogey bus alone. But even if she did, she'd have to get anything she was bringing out and onto the bus, and then those windows are huge. I've asked Will, next door, but he says she's never brought anything anywhere. I've seen you talking to him—him talking to you, rather—so I know you know he'd know."

Tom opened his mouth.

"—And before you say Will Barry can't possibly see *everything*, he's not the only Mr. McNosey in Wrinkle City."

His mouth snapped shut at this casual use of what he'd *thought* was a private post office nickname for their community.

"There's Mr. Hansen, down in unit seventeen and Theresa Prosinthal up in one-twelve. And maybe Arnie Green, in sixty-seven, would qualify. They're not as apt to gossip as Will—every time that man opens his mouth, I'm half afraid his guts are going to fall out—but they've all made a habit of knowing *everything* that goes on, whether it's their business or not."

She waved an arm, a gesture that took in all of Fernald Court. "Places like this, for some people they're like immersive-experience soap operas. Why get hooked on the flat characters you see on daytime TV, when you can get hooked on the actual lives going on around you all the time? And I happen to know Will talks with those others on a regular basis. Kind of like a loose birdwatching club that gets together to trade notes on rare sightings. If my cat-killing neighbor downstairs was making a habit of taking *anything* out of here, never mind any kind of quality antiques, William 'Snoopy' Barry would know. And he'd tell when asked. The man just can't help himself."

"Okay, fine." Tom was tired of being confused, tired of shrugging—tired of being at least one step behind in this conversation. He'd heard that old saw about a lawyer being trained to never ask a question to which they didn't already know the answer. This lady had been a lawyer, so all her questions here must be, in her mind at least, rhetorical: she already knew the answers, but was phrasing everything as questions to make a point. "Then you tell me: What's she doing with all the stuff?"

Thin shoulders rose and fell. "I haven't a clue."

Shit. So much for old saws. "All right. So what does all this mean?"

Another rise and fall. "I haven't a clue. But I don't think it's anything good. I freely admit bias, since I'm positive that old bitch killed Fluffy, but I think there's something wrong with that woman. Anyone who could do with what was done to that cat, I—" The words choked off like a fist had suddenly squeezed her throat and she shuddered. Tom remembered what old 'Snoopy' Barry had said: nothing left but a mess of fur, collar, and tail. He wondered how much this woman had seen, had needed to look at in order to make some kind of identification. Would just the collar have been enough? And even if they'd tried that, would this normally tough-as-nails woman, the terror of groundskeeping staff and neighborhood politicians alike, have *allowed* that to be enough? He rather thought she'd have demanded to see the body, or whatever was left of it.

She drew a rough breath. "Anyone who could do something like that is just evil, in my book. So now I've learned there's almost nothing *to* learn about her, and what there is just doesn't make a whole lot of sense. And that makes me nervous, living just upstairs from her like I do." She shook her head. "Hell, I don't even know where all that stuff is coming from."

"Russia," Tom said, happy to finally have something to contribute to this conversation, ethics or not. "From her uncle there who has a shop."

Mrs. Nelson's eyes widened in surprise. "She has an *uncle?*"

Tom remembered his own reaction to that news, back when he thought the cookie lady was merely in her seventies, or maybe a well-preserved eighty. "Yes? So she says, anyway."

She was looking over his left shoulder, not at anything, but lost in thought. "That *can't* be true. My God, he'd be older than ..."

"I've thought about that, too, and it *could* be. It happens. Older guys taking trophy second wives, or women just having whoops kids when they're really young, then—"

"I understand it's *possible*. Happens all the time, aunts and uncles younger than their nieces and nephews. Where do you live? Under a rock? But what are the odds there's a hundred-year-old man out there somewhere sending stuff to his hundred and nine year old niece every week?"

"Well, when you put it *that* way ..."

Her eyes were sharp again. "Do you know her uncle's name? Or where this shop actually *is?*"

"Not really. I mean, the return address, names, everything but *her* name and address, it's all in Russian. I can't even make sense of the letters. And she's *said* her uncle's name, and his town, but they both sound like a tractor trailer stripping its gears when she does. I can't remember them. Couldn't pronounce them if I could. I can barely pronounce *her* name, and that's written out for me in English."

She sank into thought. Tom did, too, but he was thinking he'd been standing there so long this was probably going to count as his break. This was not how he'd intended to spend his break. Then again, he'd never counted on hearing shit this weird about one of his customers. And whichever way it broke, something weird was going on about a customer here: either Mrs. Nelson was right, and there was something *really* strange going on with the cookie lady, far stranger than her seemingly inexhaustible supply of Goyas, or Mrs. Nelson was wrong, in which case, she was going crazy right in front of him. She might be lying, but he dismissed the idea: she was *so* serious about this it was making his junk feel a little tight, and if this was all an act, then she'd been wasted as a lawyer. She should have been in movies.

Mrs. Nelson came back from wherever she'd mentally gone. "I want you to do something for me."

Uh-oh.

"I want you to find out where these packages are coming from. Town of origin, the uncle's name, stuff like that. The name of the uncle's shop, if you can get it. If he's as old as she is—or, Christ, if he's older—he may be something of a Luddite. He *is* in the antique business, after all. But his shop, at least, might have a website. That'd make things a whole lot easier on this end."

"What's a Luddite?"

She waved a hand. "Doesn't matter. Can you do that for me."

On the surface it was a request, but there was no upturn at the end of the sentence to indicate there was any question involved. *That*, Tom thought, *was a politely phrased command*. He stood frozen a moment, mentally flailing. Finally, he said, "I ... I'll see what I can do?"

It was phrased as a commitment, but sounded like a question—the flip side of her own technique. She didn't look like she liked that, but glanced at her watch and took a quick peek around the corner again.

"We need to cut this short. Do this for me, all right?" She disappeared to the front of the building before he could formulate the proper lackluster response.

Dammit, he thought, finally trudging toward his parked mail truck, discovering the forgotten Goyas still clutched in his hand. *I'll ask around a little, but that's it. I really don't want to be in the middle of this feud.*

Chapter 8

The next morning, Tom was groggy and preoccupied. Mrs. Nelson's story had been running through his head all night, causing him to sleep poorly, and he'd found it waiting eagerly when he woke up. *A hundred and nine? And where* was *all that stuff going?* He spotted his supervisor walking across the floor, away from all the other carriers and alone—usually, there was someone at his elbow, either asking or bitching about something—and he decided to get the ball rolling.

"Hey, Paul? Can I ask you a question?"

"Certainly, Tom! And I think I know what you're going to ask. You see, when a man and woman love each other very much, sometimes his thing will stand up. Or maybe it's just that the wind is blowing. Who knows. Anyhoo, when that happens, it's called a *boner*, except in your case, where it's called a *joke*. Now, when your *joke* happens—"

"Can you just be serious for a minute?"

Paul frowned, considering. "Probably not. But I can try. What's up?"

"I—uh … If I have a customer who's trying to backtrack something registered, can we tell her where it's come from by the bar code? I mean follow it back through the computer and find out who sent it, where it came from, stuff like that?"

"Like something that came through without a return address?"

"Well, no. Not exactly. I, well …"

Shit. He'd had Mrs. Nelson's questions on his mind all this time, but never thought of a good way to ask Paul about them. He *couldn't* just hand over the nosy neighbor story; Paul would tell him to go shit in his hat, and he might actually get into trouble over it. He wasn't sure. But if someone were asking about their *own* stuff ...

"You know the cookie lady? Mrs. Preobrazhenskaya?"

"The dildo lady?"

Tom sighed. "I—yeah. Her."

At the sigh, Paul leaned away to look at him. "Jeeze, you *are* all serious today. Christ, kid, you gotta take your fucking laughs where you can get 'em in this business." They arrived at the supervisor's desk, and Paul slipped into his seat. "But okay. Yes, I remember Mrs. Preobrazhenskaya."

Tom blinked, impressed at the way the name rolled off his supervisor's tongue. She had neighbors who couldn't have pronounced it so well on a bet. "Well, Mrs. P. is kind of getting up there, and—"

"I'll say." Paul shuffled through some desktop papers, searching for something. "What's she, around a hundred now? Got to be getting close. I'm kinda surprised she's still alive, to tell you the truth."

Tom blinked again. "Wait—you know her?"

Paul looked up. "Well, yeah. I was their carrier out there at Fernald Court about twenty years ago. Eighteen? Whatever. Yes, I know Mrs. Preobrazhenskaya and her packages and her God damned cookies. What about her?"

But Tom was sidetracked. "You were her carrier twenty years ago?"

"Yeah." Paul grinned. "You think I was born at this desk? I have to go back to my little birds-and-the-bees speech? Tell you where I came from?"

"No, I just ... she was at Fernald Court twenty years ago?"

Paul squinted, pulling a long thoughtful face. "Maybe longer. She was already there when I got the route. Anyway, like I said: What about her?"

More than twenty years? Wow, maybe Mrs. Nelson's not *crazy.* "I, uh, like I said, she's getting up there. She's trying to write a letter to her uncle back in—"

"She's got a fucking *uncle?*"

"The guy sending her the stuff."

The supervisor frowned. "I ... don't remember anything about any uncle." He shrugged. "But that was two decades ago. And she's *way* up there. Could be anyone sending her stuff. She's lucky she still knows her own name."

Tom nodded. "Well, that's part of the problem. She wants to write a letter back to *whoever* over in Russia, but she can't remember the address, or the name of his shop or anything. I can't even be sure she's got the uncle's name right, because *I* can't pronounce it, and you can't read anything on those packages but *her* name. Can we track it back to where it came from, so I can at least give her the return address or something? I won't be able to give her the, you know, Russian-letter spelling or anything, but ..."

"Can't she just get it off the last package?"

"She threw the packaging away." Tom shrugged. "I don't think she anticipated forgetting the address like this. She seems kind of embarrassed about it. So, can we?"

Paul tilted his head. "Y-e-s-s-s ... I mean, we can track it backward the same way customers track stuff forward, see every transition point where it was scanned, right back to where it was accepted into the system. But if she ... she got one recently, right?"

"The other day, yeah."

"So, if that's still in the system, I can ..."

He pulled in tighter to the desk and started tapping his keyboard, slipping through menus until he came to an entry field.

"Eighty-*two* Fernald?"

Tom nodded. Paul tapped more keys, then punched ENTER with gusto. The *working* swirly appeared for a moment, and then the screen was filled with the black-and-white photo of a package, shipping label mostly filled out in the Cyrillic alphabet.

"*Voila*!" Paul moused and clicked, and the printer behind the monitor hummed to life. It spat out a single sheet which the supervisor tugged loose and presented to Tom with a flourish: a printout picture of the cookie lady's most recent package, every letter, no matter which alphabet, clear and legible.

"There you go. Everything Methuselah's mother's looking for."

Tom reached for the sheet, thinking *Can it really be this easy?* but Paul pulled it back, looking closer.

"I can tell you one thing, though. She really *must* be losing it, because whoever's sending her this shit's not in Russia."

"What are you talking about?" Tom pointed to what he assumed was the return address. "Where do you think that is?"

Paul dragged a fingertip over lines of print that looked to Tom more like crop circles than letters. "I don't know or care what *that* shit says." He tapped the rectangular REGISTERED label, with its sharp barcode. "*That's* a USPS registered code, not international. That means whatever the box may *say*, it was shipped inside the US of A."

Tom felt his eyebrows try to shake hands. "But that's ... Seriously?"

"Seriously. It's got all those border crossing stamps, but there's no original foreign shipping info on there—you know, no Russian postage or labels with our stuff just stuck on top. Unless she's getting antiques shipped from an American military base over there—of which we have none—or maybe our embassy in Moscow. We consider those US soil for the purposes of using our system."

He handed the printout over, then leaned back in his chair, lacing his fingers across his stomach with another grin.

"So, what do you think, kid? Is she somehow getting stuff sent through our own embassy? You think the embassy *knows*? You think, maybe, the dildo lady's some kind of wrinkled sparrow?"

Tom could tell by the smirk that Paul was entertaining the hell out of himself, probably bringing what he thought of as his *A-game stuff*, but Tom: A) was distracted, confused by what he'd just found out, and B) didn't have a clue what Paul was talking about.

"Huh?"

"Oh, for Christ's sake, kid. I'm asking if you think the old lady's a spy! An ancient Russian operative! I—Wow, I can't even joke with you. You need to see some movies, watch some TV. Hulu. Netflix. Something. You are seriously pop-culture deficient."

"I did just get caught up on *Punisher*, season two," Tom said, distracted by the paper in his hands, marveling that he'd gotten exactly what Mrs. Nelson had asked for. And then some. He held up the printout. "I can give this to the old lady?"

The supervisor made a quick shooing motion, as if brushing Tom away. "Sure, sure. Help Natasha write to Boris or whatever. Her uncle."

As Tom walked off, still looking at the printout, he heard Paul chuckling as he shuffled through the scattering of papers again. "I can't believe the old lady's getting weekly dildo shipments from her *uncle*! Weird people."

Chapter 9

Tom wrote a note summarizing what he'd learned from Paul, tucked it and the printed picture of the cookie lady's last package into a plain manilla envelope, and locked it into Mrs. Nelson's mailbox the next afternoon with that day's supply of Chinese food menus (Tso House, downtown, advertised relentlessly), ads for lawn care and NewPro replacement windows (the housing authority took care of both) and offers for burial plot insurance (talk about fucking vampires!). He considered the job done, his part in this weird seniors feud complete, and mentally washed his hands of the whole thing.

And then, the next day, another package for Mrs. P. showed up at Tom's case in the post office. Two, actually, both covered in Cyrillic writing, both bearing the USPS registered sticker that said, despite all the international stamps decorating the brown wrapper, they'd been shipped domestically, and both requiring signatures. One was the size of a shoebox, the other maybe four times as big, like the delivery boxes for long-stemmed roses he only saw in the movies.

"Must be the Bush Beater 2000," said Paul, tapping the larger as he walked by and chuckling as he strode away. "From her *uncle!*"

Terrific, Tom thought. He looked at the smaller of the packages and thought of Mrs. Nelson's words: *"If I tried to store four hundred pairs of shoes in my place, they'd be coming out my ass."*

"Where does she *put* them?" he muttered, loading them into the truck. Like he wanted to have *that* question—or any of the others Mrs. Nelson had raised—picking at his brain while she signed for them. *Fuck it,* he thought. *I don't want to be stuck between two feuding old ladies. I just won't think about any of this stuff when I ring her bell. Won't think about it at all.*

Chapter 10

So, of course, it was the first thing to pop into his head when he stepped into the dim, yellow-lit hallway of the cookie lady's building.

Dammit! Just think of something else.

He tried. He focused on what he was doing as he sorted magazines, letters, and ads into three of the four slots in the big wall box. He whistled as he noticed—and attempted to immediately forget—that the manilla envelope was gone from Mrs. Nelson's box, so mission accomplished, then realized he was covering "Despacito," the song that he'd been humming when he'd walked in on the argument. He forced his mind to wander as he tucked Mrs. P's bundle into his satchel to bring to the door with her registereds. Her Russian, domestically shipped though foreign-stamped, antiques. From her hundred-year-old uncle. To his hundred-and-nine-year-old niece.

His cat-killing niece.

Fuck!

He enjoyed the summer sunshine on the way back to his truck. He checked out the job the groundskeepers had done with the grass. He admired the flowers some of the residents planted and tended outside their buildings. He waved to Mr. Barry, who didn't pause in his conversation with Mr. Hansen, from down in unit seventeen (local birdwatchers meeting, perhaps?). He scooped the two registereds out of the back of his truck and did most of it again on the return trip to the building. But the whole way back and forth, it was like someone had mated the video recording of a nice summer day with a mental soundtrack featuring nothing but voices Tom didn't want to hear.

I want you to find out where these packages are coming from, said Mrs. Nelson.

I have on-call in gargle-gargle *who owns shop*, said Mrs. Preobrazhenskaya. *He send me thing I might find interesting.*

That's a USPS registered code. That means whatever the box may say, it was shipped inside the US of A.

She did it. She practically said she did it.

I'm asking if you think the old lady's a spy!

Fifty antiques a year ... four hundred items ... Where are they? I think there's something wrong with that woman. What was done to that cat ... is just evil.

Oh shut up! he thought at the voices in his head, then prayed they'd listen as he rang the bell for unit eighty-two. He started and gave a little yelp when the door popped open and the old woman stomped, gnarled and yellow, over the threshold.

"You okay?"

Strong, hard fingertips touched his forearm, strangely steadying though all they did was rest there. Within the face-covering goop, an eyebrow raised in concern. Curiosity? Both?

"I, uh ... Yeah. I ..."

A hundred and nine?

He knew he was staring, couldn't help it. The—what had Mrs. Nelson called it? Collagen?—coating her features smoothed them some, but there was no way someone could hide almost *eleven decades* under a little Vaseline. She'd have to have her head in a bucket of the stuff.

She absorbed his silence for a moment, and he wondered what might be showing on his face. He should have been saying something right then, but *what* was gone from his head. He knew the why: he had packages for the cookie lady. He needed something from her: her name on the delivery confirmation slip. There was a word for that, a word he used all the time, but it was just out of reach—an S word—but whenever he stretched for it, all he got was Amelia Nelson's voice saying *Soo-ry to hear 'bout yoor ket, so soo-ry to hear 'bout yoor ket.*

The broad face turned from his scrutiny a bit, but the eyes didn't. They squinted, became sly, and Tom's stomach was a sucking pit as he realized the Cat-Killing Cossack of Fernald Court was glaring at him suspiciously from the corner of one eye.

She did it! She did it, and I know! And she knows *I know!*

He tried to inhale—for a moment, he had the wild urge to cry *I don't know anything! I don't know* anything!—but his throat had closed to a panicked pinhole.

What was done to that cat, piped up his mental Mrs. Nelson, *was just evil. And she did it. She practically said she did it.*

Still looking at him sideways, the Cossack said, "You sure?"

She didn't *sound* evil, or even angry or accusatory. If anything, she sounded … concerned?

"I not go outside yet today. Is hot? You need drink of water, maybe? Maybe sit down? Take breather?" She still regarded him from the corner of her eye, but now he saw the normally pleasant smile had become something more friendly, almost jokingly sly.

"Come. You sit."

Those wooden fingers slipped from atop his forearm, came up under his elbow, and suddenly this little lady, barely half his size, was helping him across the hall to where the floor protruded from beneath the stairs from the first to second floors, forming a sort of deep shelf.

"No," he said. "I just—"

"Sit, sit-sit." She guided him into a little spin, as competent as any nurse who ever had to maneuver a patient, and backed him until his ass came to rest.

"Signature!" The elusive word finally popped into his mind, bursting from his mouth at the same instant. "I just need a signature." He gestured toward the two boxes still under his arm. "For these. I—"

She plucked the packages from his weak grip, depositing them on the shelf beside him before waving a dismissive hand. "Yes, yes. *Seeg-nature*. Okay, will get. But first, you sit. Take break. No worry. I not tell boss." She smiled, no teeth but wide under bright eyes, then mimed locking her lips and throwing away the key. Those hard fingers came back to pat his arm. "You wait here. Sit. Take breather. I come back with water."

She turned, and he watched those square haunches propel her toward her apartment, thankful they'd never again, to his knowledge, tried to eat that housecoat. As she disappeared though the doorway, he looked at the slip in his hand, then over at the parcels keeping him company on the shelf.

Evil? Something wrong with that woman? He shook his head with a snort. There was something wrong with one of the women in this scenario, but it wasn't the cookie lady. Mrs. Nelson had really done a number on him.

Correction: you let *her do a number on you.*

He needed to step back, look at the big picture. On one hand, here was Mrs. Preobrazhenskaya. He'd talked to her, what, about once a week for more than a year, and though it wasn't like they had deep, friendly conversations, they were cordial. They were what you expected during customer interactions. Plus cookies. She was an old lady living alone, giving out store-bought baked goods as tips for the delivery guy, and was taking care of him now like a little grandmother just because he was acting kind of weird and she was concerned. The only time she'd been anything less than that, she'd been arguing with a neighbor about that neighbor's cat shitting on her welcome mat.

Not really outrageous, when you think about it.

And no, he didn't know what she did with the things he delivered, but what of it? He didn't know what *anyone* did with the things he delivered. It wasn't his business, his problem, or his concern.

Then there was Mrs. Nelson: upset about the death of her cat, but also, it now occurred to him, probably still incensed that the cookie lady had stood up to her, talked to her that way, and sent her packing. In front of a witness. He'd thought some of the stuff she had to say was a little out there, sure, but if he took a step back, tried to look at the whole thing from the outside ... wow.

He'd had almost *no* interactions with her before she'd flagged him down, hissing at him like a character from a bad spy novel, hiding around the side of her own home, spouting weird things about Mrs. P. and calling the little woman evil. She'd said everyone at the Court had expressed condolences about Fluffy, and—when you took away the inflection Mrs. Nelson herself had put on the words—everything she'd supposedly been quoting from Mrs. P. had been just that: what you'd expect to hear from someone in that time and place and situation.

He understood she was grief stricken about her cat. Whatever had happened to Fluffy had been truly horrible, even just according to Mr. Barry's second-hand account. Grief is hard, and different people handle it differently, but starting an *investigation* into the woman downstairs, simply because she'd talked a little smack when the cat had shat—apparently more than once—on her welcome mat? Tom probably would have spouted off himself in that situation. And even Mrs. Nelson had to admit there was no way for squat little Anna to have gotten the kitty carcass up there where they'd found it.

And everything else she'd said, about her records search, how old the cookie lady really was, well, he really only had her word on all of that—and she was acting as if she were a mere half-step away from hitting the specialty shops in search of a tinfoil hat that was just her size.

He could even ignore anything too outrageous that came from Paul; the man would say anything simply to amuse himself. Take *him* too seriously, and you'd think the old woman currently fetching him a glass of water had a giant collection of oversized sex toys taking up a back room in her apartment, and the long box sitting beside Tom right then contained something called the Bush Beater 2000.

Mrs. P. motored back into the hall, a glass of water cold enough that condensation already beaded the side clutched in one rooty claw, and Tom just had to chuckle to himself. One neighbor acting weird and spouting crazy talk and his wildly inappropriate supervisor, and he'd been ready to turn this admittedly odd but obviously harmless old woman in to the cops as some kind of unnatural danger to society.

Jesus Christ, he was a gullible jerk.

"Feel better?" She held the glass out to him with a nod and a *you got this, Tiger* smile, and he noticed what was in her other hand: a packet of Goya cocoa cookies.

He returned her grin. "You know, I do. Thanks, Mrs. P."

"Good. Now, do you still need"—she raised her hands and hollowed out her voice, giving the word a sarcastic over-importance—"*seeg-nature*?"

He laughed and held up the slip and pen. "Yes, ma'am. You know the drill."

And as she bent to the task, signing with the same care she always took, a question popped into his head.

Just what the hell is *a Bush Beater 2000?*

Rob Smales

Chapter 11

For the next couple of weeks, though Mrs. Nelson was around, leading her discussion groups or going about with some of the other Fernald Court ladies, Tom never actually spoke with her. He was okay with that. She usually ignored him, even to the point of not saying hello once when her friends waved and wished him a good day. A couple of times, though, she stared straight at him, making what he thought of as *significant eye contact*, though its actual significance escaped him. Just more paranoid, bad spy novel stuff, he imagined. The cookie lady got her usual package a week, and Tom was on his guard as he left her building each day, half expecting to hear that sharp "Pssst!" but it never came.

Then, one afternoon, he found something waiting for him in Mrs. Nelson's mail box: a manilla envelope like the one he'd dropped off for her, this one curled up lengthwise and turned to show his name scrawled across the top in Sharpie.

He tucked it down in the back of his satchel. Again, no "Pssst!" awaited him outside. He finished with Fernald Court and drove away before pulling over to open the envelope—he didn't want it to look like he was just reading people's mail.

Tom—

Thank you for the photo and that information about the way registered mail works in this country.

The photo was exactly what I was looking for. I brought it around to some people I know and sent it out to others—linguists and some

Eastern language experts. Don't worry about not being able to read those packages of hers.

No one can.

I showed it to people who read Russian, Serbian, even some who know dialects not normally spoken anymore—she is a hundred and nine, who knows what she grew up with—and none could make heads nor tails of what was written on that package. We thought it was the Cyrillic alphabet—there are enough similarities that, on the surface, to people who don't use that alphabet or any version of it, it looks Cyrillic.

It's not.

Only one "word" is completely in an alphabet anyone recognizes, and even that's not an actual word, per se, for though they do agree every character in it is part of the Cyrillic alphabet, none of them know what it means. A couple of them have theorized, based on where it is on the label, that rather than a word, it's actually a name—the name of the sender, perhaps. Any further pictures you could get me of her packages, especially their shipping labels, would be of great assistance. If not, could you at least check anything incoming for the word ЕНТРАРИ, or Ентрари? Or maybe ask her her uncle's name again? That word, or name, we're looking for is pronounced Entrairi (ent-rare-ee). Does that sound at all familiar?

—A

Shaking his head, he slipped the note back into its envelope and stuck it into the pocket on the back of his lunch cooler.

That poor woman.

He shifted his truck into gear and started off for the next spot in his route. Packages coming from nowhere, filled with stuff Mrs. P. was storing in the same place. Languages that didn't exist. Whole *alphabets* that didn't exist. *Like someone could ship stuff with a return address in a made-up language without anyone either noticing or caring*, he thought, completely ignoring that he himself had been delivering stuff for more than a year with a return address that might as well have been in Martian for all that he could read it, or even identify the language or alphabet.

He pulled up to an intersection, swiped his turn signal on, and checked traffic.

Maybe I should say something.

But ... to who? And what would he say? And, really, wouldn't that just be putting himself back into the middle of something he was trying to avoid?

"Besides," he muttered, stepping on the gas and easing into his turn. "Either she's not really taking this around to linguists or whatever, in which case she's not really doing anything and isn't hurting anyone, or she is and there's a whole team of people involved in her craziness. If she's got a whole team, I'm sure *someone* will say *something* to *somebody*."

And so, with that settled—at least in *his* mind—he parked, put the whole thing behind him as best he could, and got on with his day.

Chapter 12

I n mid summer, Tom got his second look at what he'd come to think of as the cookie lady's third face: the one she wore while angry. Even as he turned the key in the wall-mounted mailbox, her door made that jack-in-the-box *pop* and she was standing at the foot of the stairs, calling up to him. "Tom! Come here. Please."

It wasn't the voice she used to say things like *There, now you have sneck,* and that *please* had clearly been tacked on as an afterthought, an attempt to soften what had just as clearly been a command. His hands worked automatically, sorting mail and credit card statements while his brain repeated *shit-shit-shit.* He closed and locked the box, pulled out the key, and for one wild moment had the thought that he could just leave. He could turn and walk out the door, maybe give the cookie lady a jaunty little wave as he did so. He imagined it, *saw* it, just like he'd imagined the cookie lady wobbling in little high-heeled shoes and whirling Fluffy around by the tail like Thor with his hammer, building up momentum to chuck the stiffening feline roofward.

But, just like then, he rejected the image. Sighing, he trudged over. "Hi, Mrs. P. Can I help you with something?"

"I till you you can hilp me with something."

Tom stopped on the bottom stair, but the old woman backed up a pace and gestured him down to her level; again, it wasn't a request, but a command, a non-verbal *front and center,* and he found himself obeying before he even thought about it. Skin crinkling at the back of his neck, he realized he must be in the exact position the formidable Mrs. Nelson had held before the nearly ridiculous figure in the yellow housecoat had begun backing her up the stairs.

Terrific.

The figure in the yellow housecoat didn't look all that ridiculous at the moment. There was no pleasant little smile, and though she wore, as always, what looked like a thick coating of Vaseline on her face, the features beneath it were hard and the eyes sharp. It was like facing a grease-smeared sledgehammer: sure, the grease was there, but it wasn't going to help if you got hit by the hammer.

"When you deliver document?"

Her voice was guttural, her accent thickened by emotion, and it took a moment for Tom to process, but once he did … nope. Not a clue.

"I'm … What?"

"You deliver document. Few days ago? Last week? When?"

Tom was baffled, and let it show. "Document? I—Mrs. P., I don't get to *see* what's in the stuff I give you. You know that, right? I—"

She waved him to silence, her mouth working without sound, either unsure what to say or simply driven beyond words. Her expression was partially obscured by the grease, but her eyes had no grease, and he saw them clearly. He'd heard the eyes were the windows to the soul, and if that were true, then, well, he was lucky the grease was there; it might have been the only thing keeping her head from bursting into flames of pure rage.

"No fit in mailbox. No package. Cardboard, uh,—" Groping for the English word, she spat something in

Russian, suggesting dimensions in front of her chest with her hands, but if she was asking about a document—

"Envelope?" Tom tried. "One of those oversized cardboard envelopes? Like a priority mail thing?"

"*Yes*!" The word sounded both joyous and savage, and Mrs. Preobrazhenskaya shuffled a half-step closer. Tom leaned away. "Document cardboard anvil-ope. You leave by my door yesterday?"

Retreat looked like a mighty fine option to Tom, but his heels were touching the stair riser behind him and his weight was on them; lifting either foot would have him sprawling. Because his only options were to either stand fast or actually lean *toward* the cookie lady, chance gave him the momentary appearance of courage as he stood his ground. "Yesterday? I didn't leave anything by your door yesterday."

Her dark eyes gleamed, and when she chuffed a single "*Huh*," a droplet fell from her chin; either she was so furious she was frothing, or internal flames had actually started melting that shit on her face. "I *knew*! I *knew* she took! She say she not, but I *knew*!"

He'd answered her question, now he just wanted to leave—but he'd still have to lean forward to unstick his feet. "Mrs. P.," he began. "I—"

"I get anvil-ope by my door yesterday, after you come. Afternoon. Mail, priority anvil-ope, like you say, but it been opened! Someone glue, but I see where cardboard torn across, before they try to fix. I *see*! I check date, postage date in corner, and it say take nine days to get here from California. *Nine days*! Something like that, it take nine days?"

"Well, no. From California? First class mail only takes three days, coast-to-coast. Priority, like you said, it's just two. Are—"

"You no leave yesterday? Day before?" Her feet hadn't moved, but she was definitely closer, and somehow, though far shorter than he, the cookie lady *loomed*. "Day before *that*?"

Tom shook no so hard he thought his cheeks flapped. "No! No, ma'am. I don't think you've gotten anything that didn't fit into your box in the last few days. Last week, maybe, but it's hard to rem—"

Bare horny feet shuffled a quick half-step to their right, and the little lady in yellow housecoat and curlers was bellowing past Tom, head thrown back, wide mouth writhing vigorously with over enunciation as she strove for perfect clarity with her English.

"So! You no deliver nothink like document this week! Deliver *last* week, but only show up yesterday, so someone *take*! Someone take *my* mail, open *my* ting! Try to sneak *back* to me, hope I no *know*. But I know! I know *who*!"

"Mrs. P." Tom turned to face her—and stepped away from that stair riser, ready now to bolt for the door like his ass was on fire, though he'd try for something a little more dignified. "I hope you don't think *I*—"

Her flattened palm chopped at his words, and she turned slightly, lowering her voice a hair and shouting at him from the side of her mouth. "I no talking to you." She turned back toward the stairs, aimed her voice *up* the stairs, and that voice rose to cracking with volume and anger. "I talking to *skeleton monkey* up there! Lady on third floor know what she do! *I* know too! She put her nose where not belong! But she gon pay!"

Despite being in the middle of an argument again, and the fear that the little Russian warrior woman might turn her attention back to him, Tom nearly laughed aloud. It may have been the literal translation of a Russian insult, or maybe her lack of American slang had forced her to be a little creative, but describing the spindly, sun-worshipping Amelia Nelson as a *skeleton monkey* seemed a brilliant combination of poetry with elementary schoolyard name-calling. Still, it *was* a postal issue she was upset about. "Oh, Mrs. P., you can call the post office to report—"

The cookie lady either didn't hear him, or didn't care. "You hear me, skeleton monkey! You! Third floor lady who can no take care of *kel*! You stick your nose in, and I *know*, and now you gon *pay*!"

Mrs. Preobrazhenskaya spun on one bare heel and stomped toward her door, housecoat fluttering, arms waving, no longer bellowing in English but muttering nonstop syllables Tom couldn't understand.

Her door slammed. Tom found himself standing, a little wide-eyed, in a suddenly silent hallway, looking at her door, up the stairs, and back again.

"Have a nice day?"

Chapter 13

Six days later, Monday, Tom received a registered for Fernald Court. It was a thick letter rather than a package, and the return address was in Cyrilic writing, but there was a line of Soviet postage stamps across the top along with a bar code sticker with more Cyrilic writing—with the American registered sticker slapped on top, as Paul had said—and it *wasn't* for the cookie lady.

It was for Mrs. Nelson.

Okay, Tom thought. *This is getting fucking weird.*

He still hadn't spoken with Mrs. Nelson since that day beside her building. Mrs. Nelson had always frightened him a little, the way she frightened the groundskeeping crew, and he'd been quite content not being the focus of her attention, especially after the crazy stuff she'd spouted during their secret conversation.

He hadn't done anything about her last note, not wanting to feed into her fantasy, or psychosis, or whatever. If she'd asked him about it, he'd have said he just hadn't had the chance yet. Now, though, he'd not just witnessed the goings-on between the two ladies, Mrs. P. had pulled him right into the conversation—and though Mrs. Nelson hadn't deigned to take part in last week's shoutfest, the cookie lady had obviously thought her nemesis was upstairs listening, and Tom had no reason to doubt her. Amelia Nelson had to know he'd been there again. Had to know he'd heard Mrs. P. call her names. Had to know *he* knew Mrs. P. was accusing her of tampering with the mail—possibly because Tom himself hadn't supplied her with more package pictures.

And now he had to go ring her bell and talk to her.

Terrific.

He felt silly and childish sneaking into their building, but couldn't help himself: dealing with one of these women was more than he really wanted to do today; the thought of being physically trapped between them as they argued made his nuts draw up tight. He opened and closed the front door as quietly as he could and ascended the stairs the same way, walking on the outer edges of the treads rather than right in the middle where they were more likely to creak, listening for the jack-in-the-box *pop* of the cookie lady's door. *Please*, he thought—he wasn't usually one for prayer, but what the hell—*let me just get in and out of here without drama. Please. This is not my fight. I just want to do my job and get out. Thanks. Uh, amen.*

It was summer, and the windows in the hallway were designed not to open—the better to heat in winter, he assumed—and the hottest air had risen to the top of the staircase. The temperature rose as he climbed, the air becoming thick and hot enough that he could feel it when he breathed, like ascending into a sauna. Sweat, once simply dotting his brow and upper lip, trickled down his cheeks like tears as he reached the uppermost landing and tapped tentatively on the door marked *84*.

He waited, letter in one hand, pen and slip in the other, forearming away eye-stinging moisture.

Nothing.

Shit.

He tapped louder, trying to take the stultifying air in sips rather than swallows, afraid it would heat him from the inside as well as out.

Still nothing.

The ground floor of the hall was eighty-five degrees, maybe as much as eighty-eight, but up here it had to be better than a hundred, and stuffy. Tom really wanted to sit down. Yes, sitting would be just fine—terrific, in fact. But there was nothing to sit on but the floor, and he had the horrible suspicion that, once all the way down there, he might not be able to get up again. He gave up on the idea of stealth and gave a good hard knock, the sound echoing down the stairs.

Let her hear, he thought, picturing the cookie lady. *Maybe she'll demand I come down there to talk to her again. Down there where it's a cool eighty-five.* He wiped a sweating forearm across his sweating face again, accomplishing nothing. He turned to leave ... but unit eighty-four's parking spot out front had had a car in it, and he hadn't seen Mrs. Nelson outside anywhere holding forth to her trapped little groups. Maybe she was asleep, or had the TV turned up so loud she couldn't hear his knock. It happened, older folks not wanting to admit they couldn't hear a damned thing and just seeing how loud they could get their TVs and radios. He didn't *hear* a TV, but maybe, if she were watching back in her bedroom or something ...

He put his ear to the door and listened. Heard something. Not TV sounds, like a show in progress or anything, but a hum. A whiny, feedback hum. Not like her cable was out—that would have been a static hiss—or an air conditioner's constant rumble, but a more organic sound that jumped around, mixing highs and lows. Actually, it was more a constant buzz than a hum, with little individual arpeggios standing out, like on TV whenever they showed a bee's nest, or maybe a cloud of ... flies.

A cloud of flies. Here, in an apartment in Wrinkle City. "Oh, shit."

Maybe he was imagining it. He *did* have a pretty good imagination. Maybe he was wrong. Maybe it really *was* just a messed-up television. Maybe—

He tried the knob. It turned. *Fuck.*

"Mrs. Nelson?" He pushed the door and stepped quietly through. "Hello? Are you—"

The smell wrapped his head like a hot, wet towel. *Oh, my God* came out "Oh, my *gurk!*" He buried his face in the crook of his elbow, trying to filter out the stink, but it was too late; it clung to the inside of his mouth and nose like cotton soaked in spoiled meat and shit. A few flies, either trying to get away from the smell themselves or merely attracted to the brighter light of the hallway, bounced off his face and chest. He fanned the air with the letter still clutched in his left hand. Flies coated the walls and ceiling, flitting this way and that through the rancid air in a cloud, their drone filling his ears—and through the thickest part of the buzzing horde, he saw Mrs. Nelson.

Head in the living room, legs trailing into the hallway to the back, she lay twisted half on her side, one arm thrown back while the other extended forward, as if rather than walking to answer his knock she'd chosen to somehow swim. She'd gained weight in her dying, the normally stylish sweats now too tight, her tanned, sun-worshipper's skin gone a mottled, bloated gray in the summer heat, and her face ... wasn't.

The front of her head yawned, from the empty sockets that had once held eyes to the raw, open hole where her nose used to be, to her mouth, stretched far wider than should have been possible, beyond anything outside of Saturday morning cartoons. Part of his mind, a flat, observing part, wondered for an instant what could have happened to cause this snakelike unhinging of jaw to let out the scream. Then he saw it wasn't so much that her lips were spread, but that they and part of her cheek were gone, baring her teeth and opening her face, letting you look, once you got past the horrible, skeletal grin and the few strings of red gristly muscle back by her jaw hinge, almost straight down her open throat in a way that might have been quite pleasing to any doctor telling her to *Say ah*. It was probably *very* pleasing to the maggots he could see in her gullet, writhing and eating, widening the meat tunnel for—

Motion caught his eye, and he looked up. He'd been moving forward when he saw her and he'd never quite stopped, drifting along in a kind of shock as he took it in. The changing angle allowed a better view through the box arch into the kitchen, and on the sill of the open window above the sink—

Thoughts and recognition happened almost instantly: the second thought formed before the first had finished, the third during the tail end of those two, and so on, all of it fleshing out, building up some serious muscle before hitting the conscious part of his mind with the crushing force of a hurled brick.

His first impression was it was a baby up there, on the sill and about to fall, little and white and helpless. Into the middle of that surged recognition of the way it moved: something about the sideways swing of the thing as it turned to look back over one shoulder, one extra-long arm reaching out, a too-narrow hand grasping the outer window ledge, and he flashed on a show he'd seen on Animal Planet; he'd only thought it was a baby because of its size, and whiteness, like brand new skin that had never seen the sun, but it was a monkey, a white monkey—white, that is, but for the darkness around its muzzle and the teeth it bared back at him. It had been going through the window when he'd caught sight of it, and as it disappeared, Tom had his second-to-last realization about the creature: that darkness was dried blood.

He fell back a step with a gasp.

But he'd unsnugged his face from the crook of his arm when he'd looked up, and the gasp sucked in a passing fly. The wriggling insect lodged in his throat, and that was all it took for the screaming-crying-vomiting part of his mind to shove all calm aside and send him staggering toward the hallway. He gagged crossing the threshold, trying to dislodge the tiny obstruction to no avail. It fluttered in there as he hit the top of the stairs, trying to free itself, and it was all too much. Nose filled with the clinging stink of decay, assaulted by the memory of the white grubs wriggling in Amelia Nelson's wide open throat just as a grown fly wriggled in his, Tom's stomach seized, bending him double. He clutched the railing and the hot pizza he'd had for lunch came out even hotter, forcefully ejecting the fly, and splashing the stairs, his shoes, and his legs. He'd worn shorts in the summer heat, and the thick hot spatter on his shins joined what he'd already seen and could still smell, and his stomach clenched again. Tom couldn't wait, couldn't stop. He had to get out, get away, wanted sunshine and fresh air and to never, ever come into this building again. He staggered forward even as his gorge rose—and his foot slipped on the puke-slick tread, sending him flying. He tried to call for help, but all that came out was "*Huarglayah*" as he vomited his way down to the second floor, somersaulting forward, sideways, and eventually backward, striking his head at least once each way. He fetched up hard against the wall on the second floor landing, slamming the back of his head one last time.

And as he lay there, the hall spinning around him now that he'd stopped rolling, his mind flashed back to Mrs. Nelson's kitchen, to what he'd seen that had caused the gasp that had started the chain of events ending with him puke covered, battered, and probably in need of an ambulance—and he had his final conscious realization.

Jesus Christ, it wasn't just white, it was bones*! That wasn't a monkey, it was a skeleton mon*— was as far as he got before everything went black.

Chapter 14

Blanket-swaddled but shivering, Tom sat on the ambulance tailgate, watching cops, firemen, and EMTs go in and out of 81–84 Fernald Court. Some of the younger-looking bitched non-stop about the heat in the hallway, lack of an elevator, and the state in which Tom had left the stairs, but one of the youngest cops (the one who looked like he'd joined the force merely to increase his doughnut access) kept glancing Tom's way, as if wishing to join him over there out of the action.

He wasn't shivering from being wet, as the onlookers probably assumed—and Christ, every Fernald Court resident had come out in the heat to stand around watching *this* live entertainment—but adrenaline overload and what was left of a healthy case of shock. When he'd come to—and he'd only been out a minute, as far as he could tell—staggering outside screaming for 911, police, and maybe the national guard, Mrs. Waterson had been there, part of one of those recently rare Mrs.-Nelson-less discussion circles. A retired nurse, she'd known at a glance Tom was A) more than a little hysterical and B) covered in human ejecta, and shouted for Mr. Turner, who'd been puttering in the front flowers, to turn the hose on him. The jet of icy water the old man had aimed Tom's way with an accuracy both gleeful and deadly had rinsed the majority of ex-pizza from his clothes and skin and slapped a bit of the shock out of him. Enough, anyway, that he was able to make some sense to Mrs. Waterson, who, though she'd likely begun her nursing career during the Vietnam War, hadn't lost a bit of her unflappable, handle-the-emergencyness. She'd pulled out a mobile phone and called 911, translating Tom's wild, somewhat rambling account into a series of brief, fact-filled sentences: there was a dead woman on the third floor, the body was in bad shape, and the young man who'd made the discovery had both been sick and fallen down the stairs and likely required medical attention. She made him sit, examined his bumped head, checked his eyes, and took his pulse, relaying information to the emergency operator using a whole bunch of terms Tom didn't understand.

That was okay. He was busy telling her about the skeleton monkey.

" ... So I looked up, and it was on the windowsill. It was only like a foot or two tall, and it was definitely some kind of monkey. I don't know what kind. I'm not a zoo doctor or anything, and I only saw it for a second before it slipped out the window. And it didn't have any fur or skin, which you usually see on monkeys, even on the internet. Maybe I could try looking at a bunch of skeleton pics, identify it that way? I don't know."

Mrs. Waterson turned and took a few steps away, gazing at Mrs. Nelson's building and still talking quietly to the operator. Tom made out a few words: " ... cranial ... impact trauma ... delirious ..."

Delirious? I—aw, shit, but ...

But he *had* taken a knock or four to the skull, maybe enough to have scrambled his brains a bit. Not that he'd imagined the skeleton monkey, fuck that, he'd seen that, but it hadn't occurred to him until that very moment that that particular portion of his story was going to sound crazy. Hell, when he stopped and thought about it, it sounded crazy to him, and he'd been there. Seen it. Bought the puke-covered T-shirt. He waved a hand at Mrs.

Waterson. "I'm not delirious. I saw, uh, what I saw *before* I hit my head or anything, and—"

The old nurse held up a finger. "Just a minute, Tom. They're on-scene." That last was said into the phone as she walked toward the main part of the road, waving the first arriving police car and ambulance over. They'd parked Tom on the back step of the ambulance and the EMT'd given him pretty much the same exam Mrs. Waterson had. Now, while the cops were waiting for the EMTs to finish, Mrs. W. strolled over to talk to them. Tom couldn't make out their brief exchange, but when both officers leaned around the old woman to stare his way, he was pretty sure *delusion*—or something like it—had just been mentioned.

Terrific.

The EMT wrapped Tom's head with some kind of compression thingie holding on three different ice packs, but pronounced this an accident Tom would walk away from.

"But not drive. Either we're taking you or someone else can drive you, but you need to stay away from heavy machinery for a while, and I'm advising you to go to the hospital for a cranial CT. I can't find anything actually broken, but impact trauma to the head isn't something to mess around with, and brother, you've got that. I don't mean to scare you, and I don't *think* there's anything going on beyond a minor concussion, but with this kind of thing, you want to be sure."

"I'll make sure he gets in to the ER," said a familiar voice, and Paul was there beside the EMT. "You can take care of her." He gestured toward the busy building, then looked at Tom. "Just dropping Susan off to get your truck out of here and have her finish your route," he said, in answer to

Tom's questioning gaze. "I'll hang around and get the real story, and then we can head off to the hospital, okay?"

"The real story?"

"Yeah. You're in uniform, so the cops called us, and Neery answered the phone. She got the rumor mill started right away."

Tom closed his eyes, feeling a pain that had nothing to do with his injuries. Neery was possibly the most excitable human Tom had ever met. If *she* was working on his story ...

Paul caught his expression. "Yeah. Before I even left, she had you busting in on a robbery in progress and taking on gun-wielding psychos in some kind of a shoot-out. Where *you* might have gotten a gun, I have no idea, but I'm sure she'll come up with something." He grinned and threw a thumb over his shoulder, toward where Mrs. Waterson spoke with another cop. "According to *that* lady, you somehow tripped on your own dick and fell down the stairs. Neery's gonna be disappointed." He looked thoughtful. "I like the gunslinger version better. Maybe I'll let her run with it for a couple of days, see what she can come up with."

The first two cops who'd shown up were suddenly standing to either side of Paul. "Sir? If EMS is done with you for now, we need to get some kind of statement from you."

Paul glanced at them, then finger-shot Tom. "I'll be around. Whenever you're done here, we can head off to the hospital, okay?" Without waiting for a response, he dropped back behind the cops and headed off toward Mrs. Waterson again. Tom watched his supervisor go—and his eye was caught by a flash of yellow at the edge of the crowd.

The police hadn't actually strung up crime scene tape like they did on TV, but they had asked people to stay back, forming a kind of invisible *do-not-cross* line out at the curb. The spectators had dutifully formed up along that line, shoulder-to-shoulder and three or four deep in places, muttering and talking amongst themselves, but there was a gap right in the middle of the crowd, about seven or eight feet wide. Right in the center of that gap, stood the cookie lady.

It was the first and only time Tom had ever seen her outside but wearing her indoor face, grease slick in the sunlight, bare toes gripping the sidewalk, canary-yellow housecoat fluttering in the breeze.

It might have been just that, that she'd been pulled from her home without being allowed to put on her public face, that was keeping her neighbors at a distance. They might have been trying to offer her a little dignity, pretending not to see her, giving her an hour or two of social invisibility ... but Tom didn't think so.

While he watched, no one even so much as glanced her way. No one gave her the side-eye, or looked at her surreptitiously before turning back to their companions to whisper behind a cupped hand about their wacky neighbor. The people to either side turned away from her to speak, but those they spoke to never turned back to them, responding from the corners of their mouths, their attention fixed on the scene in front of them. Even people passing behind were giving her a wide berth.

She has enough room to swing a dead cat, he thought.

The cookie lady, it seemed, only had eyes for Tom. Eyes that were, deep within their jelly-smeared nests, cold and hard. He'd seen her glaring like that on two previous occasions: once she'd been saying *But won't*, the other *Now you gon' pay.* He heard her voice saying those things in his head.

That same rough voice had said *skeleton monkey.*

It suddenly seemed very important that Mrs. Preobrazhenskaya not hear what he'd seen. It was silly, childish—as silly and childish as creeping into the building to avoid being caught between two arguing old ladies—but the feeling was at least as strong, and not to be denied.

"Sir?"

He started to turn back to the waiting cops—and saw a single figure whose attention was fixed firmly on something *other* than Tom. Will Barry stood at the edge of the crowd, the face beneath his ever-present fishing hat turned almost in profile to Tom, gaze apparently trained on Anna Preobrazhenskaya. A quick glance showed the cookie lady hadn't moved a muscle, and he turned back to Mr. Barry, the three of them forming a weird triangle: Tom looking at the old man, who stared at the old woman, who, in turn, glared at Tom. As if sensing his gaze, the ex-reporter darted his eyes in Tom's direction, blanching when he saw he was being observed. He whirled and moved away quickly, almost scurrying toward his building.

Where's he going? Tom wondered. *The guy who wants to know everything around here is walking away from* this?

"Sir?" the cop said again, and Tom moved toward him, trying hard to be unaware of the stocky yellow shape in his peripheral vision but failing. He told of the registered, of knocking on the door, of assuming Mrs. Nelson was just in there watching TV. When he got to the part about hearing the flies through the door, the younger officer, one of the cops who'd complained about the heat and the state of the stairs, wrinkled his nose in distaste.

The older of the two took notes and asked occasional quiet questions, but when his story reached the point when Tom was backing away from the body and heading for the stairs, the younger officer broke in.

"Why did you back away right then, sir? Did you see anything unusual? You know, out of place? Maybe weird?"

The older cop went perfectly still at his partner's question. His expression didn't change—his deadpan eyes hadn't varied at all, that Tom had seen, since they'd gotten there, the fabled *cop face* in action—but Tom still got the impression he didn't approve of the interruption.

The younger cop, on the other hand, couldn't suppress his eagerness to hear Tom's answer, and any small doubts Tom had harbored about Mrs. Waterson mentioning his *delusions* disappeared like a coin from a street magician's closed fist. This young man with the badge couldn't wait to get back to the station, or maybe to the local after-shift bar, and tell his buddies about the whacko they'd interviewed that afternoon at Wrinkle City.

Though he'd tried to tell Mrs. Waterson about it, his head was on a little straighter now. He knew what he'd seen, but there was no way these two were going to believe it; one had the eyes of a modern-day Joe Friday, interested in just the facts—those that made sense, anyway—while the other was looking at him like he was that afternoon's entertainment. Besides, there was that looming yellow shape he was trying so hard not to look at.

"Oh, I don't know." Tom looked hard at the younger cop. "The huge swarm of flies was unusual, I guess. Or maybe that her face was gone?" The officer's eyes changed, losing their anticipatory gleam. This was not the answer he'd been looking for, and he was getting it in a tone he hadn't expected. "Yeah, that might have been a little weird for me, that her eyes and nose were missing. Christ, even her *lips* were—"

"All right," said Officer Cop Face. "So you started for the stairs. That's it?"

"It's not that unusual." Young Cop's tone was a little sulky. "Looks like she's been down a few days, and she had at least one cat. The empty food and water bowl are in the kitchen. Happens a lot. Time goes by, pets get hungry, there's meat lying there on the floor—"

"I said *all right*," said Cop Face, and Young Cop subsided. From the older cop's tone and the younger one's chagrined expression, Tom suspected someone was going to be getting a talking-to once they were in the privacy of their cruiser, and he felt a tiny dark satisfaction about that. But, mentioning the skeleton monkey or no, there *was* something he could help them with.

"Mrs. Nelson's cat's been gone for weeks. Maybe she hadn't gotten around to getting rid of the food bowl and stuff, but Fluffy wasn't in there with her."

"Cats come back," said Cop Face. "I'm sure—"

"Not this one. Fluffy had some kind of an ... well, she ... You know, there's a guy in the next building, Mr. Barry, who knows all about it. You should get the story from him. He makes a point of knowing what's going on around here." He lowered his voice. "He's kind of a talker."

Cop Face's eyes finally changed, brightening a bit. "Say, Steve?"

Young Cop looked up. "Yeah?"

"Why don't you look around and find this Mr... ." He looked at Tom.

"Barry. Over in unit eighty-five. I just saw him heading that way."

"Mr. Barry. If he's not in unit eighty-five, he's probably in this crowd somewhere. Find out whatever he can tell us about the cat, Mrs. Nelson, or anything else he can think of."

Steve's face was pinched. "Seriously? But Bill—"

"Seriously," said Cop Face. "Everything. Be thorough."

Steve's shoulders slumped, but without another word he trudged toward the line of spectators, pulling out his own notebook. Cop Face—Bill—turned back to Tom and held out a card. "Thank you for your time, sir. We may be in touch if we have further questions, and if you think of anything else, anything at all, please give us a call. Now, I believe you were heading off for a CAT scan?"

The officer started back toward his cruiser, and Tom looked around for Paul. His supervisor had been watching for the police to leave, though, and was already moving Tom's way, face stretched in a wide smile. Before Tom could say he was ready to go, that smile split and words fell out in a happy shout.

"Skeleton monkey, huh? Neery's gonna shit a fucking *brick* when she hears this, she's gonna be so pissed she didn't think of it herself. I mean, I seem to recall welcoming you to the wonderful world of weird, but come on! Overachiever!" His gaze went distant as he drew near. "I'm still curious how far she can go with the whole *blazing gun battle* thing, though, so—"

Tom was horrified. "Where did you hear that? About the"—he dropped into a stage whisper—"*the skeleton thing?*"

"That lady over there's giving the story to that guy." Paul pointed to Mrs. Waterson and Mr. Hansen. "I just listened in."

Shit. Mrs. Nelson had been right about at least one thing: Mr. Barry wasn't the only Mr. McNosey here at Wrinkle City. And if Mr. Hanson had made the scene, coming all the way up from unit seventeen with his walker, then it was almost a certainty Will Barry, the professional snoop who lived just next door, had already ferreted out everyone who'd been there when Tom had staggered out of the building and squeezed every drop of information out of them. Hadn't Tom sent the cops to the old man for just that reason? It looked like Officer Steve was going to have that story to tell his post-shift drinking buddies after all, and Mrs. Preobrazhenskaya ...

He looked to where he'd last seen the cookie lady, but though the gap in the crowd was still there, there was no sign of the yellow housecoat. Had she heard Paul? Did it really matter, with the story probably circulating through the crowd even now?

"Let's go get you checked out." Paul started to clap Tom on the shoulder but paused, hand hovering, nose wrinkling. "You think maybe we could get a new blanket from somewhere? I'm not sure I want you actually touching my seats. You're a little, uh ... You're kind of, uh ..."

Tom, urgent to get the hell out of there, still took a moment to sigh. "I smell?"

"Like you wouldn't fucking believe."

Chapter 15

The CT scan didn't rule out concussion, and the ER doc, a tall youngish woman whose name Tom never quite got—Margoulos, Margoules, something like that—did tap the lump on the back of Tom's head, both on the image and in the flesh (and, dammit, that had *hurt*), and say "Yeah, this is a good one."

So he was going to have a headache for a while, and she repeated the advisory against driving or operating any heavy machinery for a couple of days. "This,"—she palpated the knot on the back of his skull again; *What is it with doctors squeezing the shit that hurts?*—"is right over your occipital lobe, the vision center in the brain, and your occipital lobe didn't really like it. It might not complain, but if it *does*, you could have some blurred vision or light sensitivity."

Tom was more concerned with the rest of him. He had bands of bruises over his arms, legs, and back from where they'd impacted the stair edges on his way down—and, of course, Dr. Mar-whatsis had to poke and squeeze each one—but most concerning (and baffling) to him was that his left testicle hurt, and seemed a little swollen.

"Just how the hell did you fall down these stairs?" she asked, giving him a gentle probe that about sent him scooting off the exam table.

In the end, she sent him home with orders to rest, avoid lots of movement for the next day or two, take Tylenol every four hours, and get an ice pack on his swollen nut.

"A lap full of frozen peas ought to help out with that bad boy," she'd said, pointing to his crotch. "That's what we tell our vasectomy patients; it'll work for you, too."

Paul had gone ("Hey, I gotta see how Neery's story's shaping up!"), taking Tom's keys to handle ferrying his car home for him, so Tom got an Uber. They stopped at a grocery store, where he hobbled into the frozen foods section, then hobbled out again carrying three bags of peas—they were on sale. The woman running the register, a matron who could have lived at Fernald Court herself, took one look at Tom's gait, one at the register belt full of frozen veggies, and had tipped Tom a knowing nod. "These should fix your plums up a treat," she bellowed in her *I'm not so old I can't hear, y'all are just a bunch of mumblers* voice. "When my Danny—God rest his soul—had his vasectomy, a couple of bags of these had him up and about in no time. And the best part is"—she dropped into a rusty stage whisper that was somehow louder than her normal shout, adding a wink that made Tom shudder—"it doesn't take any of the lead out of your pencil, if you know what I mean."

She resumed her everyday bellow. "Will that be cash or charge, hon?"

Tom ran his debit card through the reader, silently wishing the old woman a stroke.

Chapter 16

Back at his apartment, his keys were in his mailbox. Paul had called to tell him they were there—and that Neery's story was shaping up nicely—so his car was out front somewhere, but he was too damned tired to go looking for it now. He tottered carefully up to the second floor, let himself in, and called the office. He told Martin, the clerk who picked up, that no, he did not, in fact, own a .44 Magnum, and left a message for Paul concerning his medical status: he was going to be out of work for the next day, maybe two. Martin took down the message, dutifully repeated it back to him, then said, "Hey, before you go, can I ask you a question?"

Tom sighed. "Sure."

"That cigarette case, the one that deflected the bullet that would have pierced your heart: was it silver or steel? And where can I get one of those babies, because I've been thinking I might start—"

"Just make sure Paul gets that note, okay?" Tom hung up. "Fucking Neery."

He bow-leggedly pushed the coffee table closer to the couch so he could put his feet up while facing the TV—he'd never been one of those *you have to have a recliner* guys, but now he was seeing the appeal—threw two-thirds of his recent purchase into the freezer, shucked his shorts, scooped up the remote, and sat down in his boxer-briefs to get to know his bag of peas a little better. The cold was a shock at first, and in a place where he least appreciated such, but after a while he had to grudgingly admit both the young doc and old register woman had been correct: his pained bits *did* feel somewhat better.

He still wished death on that cashier, though.

He tried to watch something, thumbing the remote through Netflix, Prime, and Hulu, but nothing held his attention for more than a few moments. Without cops asking him questions, Paul yammering in his ear, a doctor squeezing anything that might hurt, or an old woman yowling out a very personal conversation in a very public place, he really had nothing to distract him but himself ... and himself seemed to be filled with shit he really didn't want to think about.

Mrs. Nelson had had no face.

That was a biggie. Whenever he realized he had absolutely no idea what was happening on the screen before his eyes, it was because the one behind them was rerunning his trip through the door at eighty-four, zooming in again and again on the empty sockets, the bared teeth, the missing cheek.

The whole *seeing right through the side of the face* thing had seemed pretty cool in *Jonah Hex*. Seriously bad-ass. In real life, though, with the red meat-strings forming a ragged curtain for you to peek through and see those throat maggots squirming—

He got up to swap his warming bag of peas for some freshies from the freezer, needing the physical activity to help break his train of thought, tossed the used bag back in there to refreeze, glanced at his kitchen window ... and that *other* thing came creeping into his thoughts.

The skeleton monkey.

It wasn't possible, but he'd seen it. It couldn't have been real, but he'd *seen* it.

He had a vivid imagination, sure, but this hadn't looked like anything that might have come out of *his* head. All *his* experience with walking dead things was of them being gross and horrory. Shuffling bags of rot, like in *The Walking Dead*, or if they were older, had been, you know, buried awhile, in some Romero movie or something, there were bits of gristle and stuff hanging from the bones. Moss and shit, at least!

But this thing had been so white, so clean—except for the blood, and that had come from Mrs. Nelson. When he pictured it, he thought of this old *Jason and the Argonauts* film he'd seen with his dad when he was a kid. It was from the fifties or sixties, and the monsters had all been done with this horrible stop-motion process that had quit looking real to him by the time he was eight, but the skeleton soldiers the hero had fought came out of the ground looking clean and polished. *The fifties and sixties probably had tight-assed rules about gore*, he thought, rolling through the countless thumbnails on Netflix again without even seeing them.

The skeleton monkey had looked white, and clean, and polished. Except for its mouth. *It's just a messy eater.* He grimaced.

It had been clean and polished, yes, but there had been nothing stop-motiony about the way it moved. He'd recognized it in part because of the smoothly simian way it had shifted, fast and light. He'd only seen it for that one second, but it had been enough to tell him he'd have thought it a real live monkey if he hadn't been close enough to see its ribs. Its lipless teeth and eyeless sockets, so much like Mrs. Nelson's, though its sockets had been clean and dry while hers were … not.

And let's face it, he thought, *the phrase* skeleton monkey *popped into my head so easily because I'd heard it recently.*

He'd been trying not to think about that because he knew on an instinctual level it would lead him into some weird, seriously horror-movie shit.

Like I'm not *in the middle of some weird horror-movie shit already?*

On the coffee table by his calf, his phone rang.

Tom jumped, flinching when his testicle throbbed. "Christ!" He scooped up the mobile and checked the screen, but didn't recognize the number. *Probably Paul, looking for more of the* real *story*, he thought, accepting the call. *Or Neery, looking to complain about it.* "Hello?"

It wasn't either Paul or Neery. "Tom? You're in danger!"

Chapter 17

"What? Who is this?"

"It's Will Barry. You saw it, and she knows you saw it. She knows, Tom, and—"

"Mr. Barry?" The old man was talking far too fast and didn't sound quite right. Was that ... panic? "Hold up. How did you get my number? And what are you talking about? Who knows? Knows what?"

"I found your number back when I found your address for the Christmas card. I've just never needed it before. But look, that's not important right now. You're in danger, and—"

"Mr. Barry, please. It's been a long, shitty day, and I don't have the patience for riddles or mysterious warnings, so just ... just slow down. Who knows what, and how am I in danger?"

"I'm trying to tell you, if you'll *listen*! I know you saw the skeleton thing, and Anna Preobrazhenskaya knows too!"

The chill in Tom's scrotum suddenly had nothing to do with peas. "What are you talking ab—"

"I know you were working for Amelia. I was too. Where do you think she got all her information about Anna?"

"Investigating," Tom said without thinking, only partially aware he was confirming he even knew what the old man was talking about. "She still knew people, and—"

"*I* still know people, kid! Amelia was a lawyer, for a big firm. Those lawyers don't do their own legwork. They hire investigators, and that's what Amelia did with me."

Tom wasn't really sure how fast all this was going, but to his whirling head it felt *fast*. "Wait, wait. She said *she* was—"

"After the cat thing, Amelia hired me to look into Anna. I've always been a *little* curious about her. I mean, let's face it, she kind of stands out. I know I'm regarded as the neighborhood snoop, but that's just talking to people. I don't usually all-out *spy* on my neighbors, though. But Amelia was paying, so ..."

"But Mrs. Nelson said—"

"She said what I asked her to say. We were doing kind of a confidential informant thing. Not like Anna couldn't have figured it out, but it'd take her a little while to *know*. Give me a little warning, maybe."

"But—"

"Look, Amelia said she took your photo to a bunch of linguistics experts, right? Well, she gave that photo to *me*, and *I* took it to a bunch of people."

That chill in Tom's scrotum solidified into ice. There were dead bodies and blood-faced skeleton thingies in his life at the moment, but *this* was something he understood, a real life thing, and his fear grabbed onto it like a lifeline. He'd not felt right about giving that picture to Mrs. Nelson, and he'd thought she'd be the only one to know. Now *another* customer knew he'd shared pictures of one of his people's mail—and it was the biggest blabbermouth in town. People were definitely going to find out. Could he get in trouble for that at work? How much?

"Look, Mr. Barry, about that picture—that was a one-time thing, and not something I'd ever—"

"What? You're not listening! Kid, you are in *trouble*, and it has nothing to do with anything but that *you saw that skeleton thing*!"

The raw emotion in the old man's voice cut through Tom's mental fog. "What I saw—"

"I know what you saw. I've seen it too. Look, Amelia came to me after the cat thing—she and Anna'd had some kind of confrontation about it, and she'd gotten serious about getting back at her. She hired me, and I started investigating Anna. I was watching her. I found out some stuff—some so strange I didn't even tell Amelia. It was too far-fetched."

"Worse than a hundred and nine year old woman getting weird packages covered with a language that doesn't exist?" Tom said, in a combination of sarcasm and disbelief.

"You saw that skeleton thing, kid." Mr. Barry sounded annoyed. "You tell me."

Tom nodded. "Okay. Fair point."

"I can take a guess what Amelia told you. The shipments, no place to keep them, and that old bag really *is* old, a lot older than she looks. All that sound familiar?"

"Yeah, but what's all that got to do with ... anything I might have seen this afternoon? And what goddamned danger am I supposedly—"

"Wait!"

Silence.

"Hello? Mr. Barry? Hello?"

Will Barry's voice was a harsh whisper. "Hang on, kid. I ... Shit. I'll call you back. I hope."

The phone beeped in Tom's ear as the call disconnected. He stared at the screen for a moment. "You've got to be fucking kidding me."

He held the phone for a while, waiting for Mr. Barry to call him right back. No dice. He tossed the phone on the coffee table, looked down at the cold bag of peas slowly sogging its way through his boxer-briefs, and a sound burst out of him, right up from the chest, an explosive cross between a laugh and shout of horror.

"*Cha!* Okay, this is fucked up."

Fuck it. The old guy had called *him*—he didn't have to run to Will Barry's timetable. He picked up the phone and rang back the last incoming call. It went straight to voicemail. He hung up.

Shit! All right, all right. He turned off the TV and closed his eyes. His natural inclination was to be imaginative; his friends called it *gullible and dipshitty.* Since the start of this thing, he'd been making an effort to act more like an adult than the kid he so often felt like, to be more skeptical and real-world focused.

Mrs. Nelson had been very real-world focused. Now she had no face.

Don't be that guy. Don't be the skeptical asshole—that guy'll get you killed. What's gullible, dipshitty me think about all this?

Gullible dipshitty Tom leapt at the challenge like Augustus Gloop turned loose in Willy Wonka's chocolate room, pointing out three facts right quick: Mrs. P. had been angry with Fluffy the cat, and Fluffy had died horribly; Mrs. P. had been angry with Amelia Nelson, and Mrs. Nelson had died horribly; and that afternoon, the cookie lady had glared at him with that same icy gaze he'd only seen in connection with Fluffy and Mrs. Nelson. And then Mr. Barry had called to tell him he was in danger.

Fuck.

But seriously, skeptical Tom broke in. *She's kind of weird, but she's just an old lady.*

An old lady, gullible Tom shot back, *who fucking shouted* skeleton monkey!

Tough for skeptical Tom to get around that one. Because even ignoring Mr. Barry's call, if someone suggested he'd simply imagined the skeleton monkey—his mind, in a moment of severe stress, latching onto the phrase from his subconscious—well, *something* had gnawed on Mrs. Nelson's face. Tom hadn't imagined that; Officer Steve had remarked on it. He'd blamed the cat, but Tom knew better. And the building had been swept for rats after what had happened to Fluffy. Mrs. Nelson had seen to it. So, in the absence of cats, or rats, that just left ... what?

I talking to skeleton monkey up there! Lady on third floor know what she do!

He'd thought the cookie lady was talking to Mrs. Nelson at the time—ostensibly speaking to Tom, but yelling so the woman upstairs could hear her name-calling—but what if she hadn't been? What if she'd been doing just what she said, and talking to the skeleton monkey already lurking in the upper portions of the building? Telling *it* the lady on the third floor knew what she'd done? Telling *it* she had to pay?

Now you're just being silly, the (so-called) rational part of his brain said.

That's what you said about Mrs. Nelson, he told the rational, skeptical voice. *And look what happened to* her.

He waited a bit, but skeptical Tom didn't seem to have anything to say to that.

Good. Because it's been a long fucking day.

He called Mr. Barry again. Voicemail. He limped to the fridge—he *was* moving and feeling a little better—and tossed the thawed bag of peas back in the freezer. Thawing and refreezing may make them inedible, but Tom was of that opinion about peas anyway, and it sure wouldn't hurt their therapeutic value. He grabbed that third bag while he was in there. Why make another trip few minutes later?

You're in danger! said his brain, in a fair approximation of Mr. Barry's panicked tones. *You're in trouble, and it has nothing to do with anything but that you saw that skeleton thing!*

"Shit."

He was on the second floor, but, then, Mrs. Nelson had lived on the third while Fluffy had been found on the roof. His apartment wasn't very big—kitchen, bathroom, living room, two bedrooms—and he scooped the phone from the coffee table and limped from room to room closing and locking windows, and damn the summer heat without any cross breeze. He waited for that skeptical voice to pipe up while he took a couple of window-ledge fans down so he could close and lock the double-hungs, but he never heard a dissenting word.

Apparently, even skeptical Tom remembered the look that had been in Mrs. Preobrazhenskaya's eyes.

He stopped in his bedroom, looking at the air conditioning unit chugging away on the windowsill. It was one of the smaller ones, the right size to cool his room at night and not much more, and on any other day he might have popped it out to set on the floor in the corner, easy-peasy, but ...

Just the thought of lifting the thing out of there made his testicle twinge.

Fuck it, he thought. *No little monkey, especially one without any muscle mass at all, is going to move that out of there.* Especially *not clinging to the outside of the building like some fun-sized Spider-Man.*

The unit had accordion-style wings on the sides, filling the rest of the window gap, and he'd screwed them straight into the bottom of the old wooden sash, locking them open and attaching the unit itself directly to the window; no one was pulling that machine loose or lifting the window higher to let gravity do it for them.

The door was locked, windows the same, and this one was plugged with a practically immovable object. Nothing was getting in here. Not without breaking a window, and at least then he'd hear it coming.

And it's not like you live just upstairs from the woman, either. Even if she did *have anything to send after you—a skeleton monkey perhaps—how would she know where to send it?*

That sounded suspiciously like skeptical Tom, but if it was, he was at least trying to be helpful.

I'll think about it in bed, he thought, taking his last dose of Tylenol for the day (adding in one extra tablet, because, you know, still-sore nut). *It's not like I'm going to get a lot of sleep with all this on my mind anyway.* He put the phone on the nightstand and turned off the lights, then the air conditioner—the room was already pretty cold, and he had a ceiling fan—just in case. If something somehow *did* break a window in the night, he wanted to hear.

Mrs. Nelson's faceless face drifted through his thoughts as he settled that last Birdseye bag into place. Yeah, he definitely wanted to hear.

Jesus, he thought as his head hit the pillow, his body exhausted but his mind thrumming. *I'll just wait for Mr. Barry to call back.*

And then the darkness swallowed him up and he knew no more.

Chapter 18

Tom's eyes popped open, looking up at the white ceiling, now gray in the dim. He half-rolled, reaching for the phone at his bedside ... but no, the screen was dark, no call coming in or missed calls showing. He scooped it up to check, but the Samsung had nothing to tell him but the time: 3:09 am. It hadn't been Mr. Barry finally calling. He dropped the phone and lay back, mentally replaying everything that had happened since he'd opened his eyes, then trying to go a touch further, into the moments before he'd awoken, but failing. *Something* had roused him, but what—

Scratch. Scritch-scratch.

His breath froze. Everything he had, all his focus, was suddenly in his ears, listening for a repeat of—

Scritch-scratch, scritchy-scratch.

Wide eyes widened further and air whistled in through a throat constricted so tight Tom could have choked on fog as he followed the sound to the window, to the accordion panel to the left of the air conditioner, and—

Scritchety-thunk.

And the air burst out of him in another cross between a laugh and shout of horror, this one drawn out with relief, a "Chaaaaaaaahhhhhhhh ..." with a little "ha-ha" tacked onto the end.

No wonder he'd not woken panicked; he'd recognized the sound in his sleep quicker than he had awake. Birds. It was frigging birds nesting by his air conditioner again.

With a grunt of reawakened pain, he rose from the mattress and limped two steps to the air conditioner. His head and neck hurt worse than his *plums*, as the deaf old cashier had called them—she'd been right, those frozen peas seemed to have fixed him up a treat—as did all the body bruises he'd gotten from the stairs, but he was a man, and certain injuries would always be babied, no matter how minor. He reached out and flicked a finger against the plastic extender panel.

"Ha! Get the fuck out of there!"

He listened for a flurry of wings, the feathered equivalent of shouting *Holy shit!* and ducking for cover—and, come to think of it, it should be a loud fluttering. That last *thud* had been a good one. No thrush or sparrow made that kind of bump. Pigeon perhaps?

Silence.

Tom imagined the bird—he'd made it a pigeon—standing frozen on the other side, head cocked at that odd angle particular to avians and old folks, focusing one round eye on the wall that had just banged and spoken to him. He tapped harder, knocking with a knuckle.

"G'wan! Fuckoff!"

Silence.

Wait. Do pigeons not fly at night? He looked at the bedside clock. 3:11 am. *Wait again. Don't pigeons* sleep *at night? I think they do. So would one* really *be building a nest right n—*

The accordion panel snapped aside like a tiny folding door, and two things struck Tom simultaneously: one, the *frame* around the accordion panel was screwed to the sash but all that held the panel in place was the clip holding it to the end of that frame; and two, that was no pigeon.

A nearby streetlight teamed up with the moon to make it brighter outside than Tom's shaded and curtained room, so at first what he saw was mostly silhouette: the cage of the ribs, the thin shapes of the arm bones, thickest where they joined at elbow and wrist, one limb raised to hold back the plastic panel. But the moonlight glinted atop the smooth rounded skull, and within the eye sockets, invisible that afternoon during his daylight glimpse but showing quite nicely in the gloaming, a pair of tiny blue flames burned at an impossible internal distance, matches viewed through the wrong end of a telescope.

Tom inhaled to scream, but the tiny figure acted first. The other clawed hand came up, clutched the plastic frame, then the thing reared back, mouth stretched wide to bare two-inch fangs, and used its arms to slingshot itself into a leap straight at Tom's face.

Tom reacted with a speed born of terror, lashing out with the only weapon he had: he flung the thawed and soggy bag of peas he'd held since rising as hard as he could. The Birdseye bag struck the monkey thing with a wet slap just inches from Tom's releasing hand, the force of a pound of soft clinging veg reversing the creature's trajectory—it was only bones, and not quite two feet tall, after all, how heavy could it be?—sending it tumbling back through the open panel. A claw flashed out, catching the frame as it passed through, and the thing was back where it started, clinging to frame and panel with one hand and both feet, the other hand tearing away the burst and clinging plastic bag. Hanging outside the window rather than standing in it, Tom could see the thing better in the moonlight. It might have looked funny, lumpy with glommed and clinging peas, but the quick and sinuous way it moved—a country mile from the stop-motion monsters it had earlier put him in mind of—made his guts go cold, and the burning little pinpricks of its eyes, unblinking and focused only on him, caused his bowels to go slack.

Nothing funny here.

The thing reared back and leaped again. Tom flung himself sideways. It had the far greater distance to cover—all he had to do was duck—but it moved with shocking quickness, and he was almost too slow: a single talon burned a quick line of blood across his cheek, just beneath his left eye.

With a cry, Tom spun away, knowing he had to get through the door and slam it behind him. He wore only boxer-briefs, and every inch of exposed skin made him feel more vulnerable. A yard away, the skeleton monkey landed on the bed with a soft *flumph*. Tom started for the door, nearly sobbing when he realized he'd closed the damn thing to keep the cool air in even though he'd turned the AC off. He'd have to get there, pull the door open, get through, turn, and yank the door closed. There were too many steps, it would take too long, and he'd seen how fast that little fucker moved. There was no way he'd—

A rustling came from the bed, and even in his extremity, frantic motion caught Tom's eye. The thing had landed amid a rumpled mound of cast-aside sheet rather than a smooth surface, and the loose fabric had caught on a couple of those sharp little finger and toe bones, like a kitten first walking on a carpet and getting its claws caught in the nap. It would be free in an instant, but at the sight of it, Tom's adrenaline-charged body acted before the idea had fully registered in his mind. Passing the foot of the bed on his way to the door, he reached out and gave the sheet a hard yank, pulling the feet out from under the monkey thing, then flipped the material up and over, like trapping it in a net. It would only slow the thing for a few seconds, but a few was better than none, and it just might be enough.

Off-balance from grabbing and throwing the sheet midstride, he hit the door with his shoulder to stop his headlong run. He grabbed the doorknob, twisted and pulled, just as, behind him, cloth tore with a series of jagged purrs, and there was another light thud. He swung himself around the door, hanging from the knob like a monkey himself with one hand as he sought the outer knob with the other. His room came onto view as he spun, a cat-sized shadow shooting toward him from the darkness beside the bed. He caught the outer knob, released the inner, and jerked his hand through the gap just in time. The door slammed hard. His own weight popped his fear-sweaty grip loose from the knob and sent him sprawling backward. The banging door sounded a one-two beat, as the little thing of bone struck the closed portal just a quarter-second too late: even with the tangling sheet to contend with, it had still almost made it through.

"It's so fucking fast," he whispered, then wheezed, every band of bruising across his back pointing out in no uncertain terms that, second to falling down the stairs again, being thrown back against the hard floor was their least favorite thing to do.

He sat, gasping, for a moment—then the loud scrabbling of clawed finger bones at the other side of the door—not just scratching at it, but *attacking* it—sent him scrambling backward. The door shuddered in its frame as the creature inside went into a frenzy, raking and beating at the wooden panel.

It can't get through, can it?

But this wasn't a solid wooden door, like the front and back doors to the apartment, but a cheap interior panel installed by a landlord looking to keep the overhead low. It was a hollow or foam core, the kind of thing meant to offer privacy and maybe trap air conditioning, but not much else. It certainly wasn't designed to keep an intruder out, or even a twenty-inch crazed attack skeleton in.

I don't know what that thing is, but if it's anything like the zombies in the movies, it's not going to get tired, and it's not going to quit. It'll get through there eventually, but at least I've got time.

As if in response to the thought and trying to prove him wrong, the scrabbling, scratching, clawing attack ceased. Tom leaned into the sudden silence, listening hard—then jumped as the door rattled once, a quick jiggle.

What's it do—

The doorknob shook, jerked, and turned, a little in one direction, then the other, back and forth.

The fucking thing's working the knob!

That wasn't a dog or a cat he'd trapped in there. It was bones, but it was *monkey* bones, and that meant little hands. It was likely hanging from the inner knob just as Tom had, and the only thing keeping it from opening the door right away was the lack of flesh on those tiny fingerbones, the smooth metal knob slipping through those naked phalanges. But it would get out, Tom was sure, and much quicker than clawing its way through.

"Time to go!"

Part of Tom pointed out that he could go back and hold the door shut—there was no lock, but he could at least grip the doorknob and keep it from turning—but all Tom wanted was to get away from the monkey thing, far away, and right fucking now. He flipped over to his hands and knees, crawling for a moment before lurching to his feet, scooping up his discarded work shorts from beside the couch on the fly. He'd grabbed them purely through reflex—he was going out, some part of his mind said, he needed more than just his undershorts—but as he felt their heft and heard a jingle, he realized they still had his wallet and keys in the pockets.

One stop shopping for getting the fuck out of Dodge, he thought, dashing for the front door, bruises and delicate teste be damned. He nearly dislocated his shoulder when he yanked the knob and it didn't open, remembered the deadbolt and gave it a twist. From behind came a click, creak, and thud.

It's coming!

He jerked the door open just enough to slip through. Looked back. The bedroom door was still slowly swinging even as a small shape hurtled across the living room, arm and leg bones churning, eye sockets burning.

Fast! So fast!

He kept his grip, afraid it might not latch but bounce wide. He needn't have worried: the door slammed, and he cried out at the impact of the thing on the other side. This time, though, there was no scratching, clawing attack on the wood; immediately following the thud, the knob came to life beneath his palm, jiggling and twisting, flinging itself about like a tantruming child.

Jesus! It learned! It never even went for the door, but jumped right for the knob!

Tom clamped down, holding this door shut as he hadn't the other, surprised at the twisting force the thing generated. It couldn't overpower his hold—not yet—but it was far stronger than anything so small had a right to be.

It's not like it's using muscles *to move, fuckball!*

Right now it was a stalemate, but eventually, Tom would tire. The thing in there was strong and fast and, if Tom were right, *wouldn't* get tired. He was holding the knob lefty, and dropped the shorts to take a grip with his surer, stronger right hand. They landed with a jingle.

Right! My keys!

Holding the door righty, he bent to fish the keyring free, but with the shorts flapping loose, the damned things caught and tangled inside the pocket. He eventually thought to step on the hem and pulled the pocket inside out, and seconds later he had the key in the deadbolt and was twisting it.

At the snap of the lock, the knob went still. Tom stuck the key in the doorknob lock and twisted that as well; the deadbolt was controlled on the inside by an easy-to-twist knob, but the doorknob lock was one of those little nubby-twisty center buttons.

Let's see you get hold of that *with those little bones, fucker!* he thought, his face spread in a wide smile that didn't feel like his own. A brief giggle escaped him, a quick "Hee-hee."

Hysterical. I'm hysterical. Got to calm down. Gonna lose my shit. Got to keep it together.

"Everything okay?"

Tom whirled, a little scream escaping at the new voice. The smile dropped off his face, and he had no idea what replaced it, but whatever it was made Mrs. Green, his neighbor across the hall, recoil.

"Hi." He tried for bright and friendly, but thought he might sound manic.

"*Is* everything okay, Tom?" Mrs. Green asked again, looking at him a little sideways, tone cautious and eyes narrowed, as if worried the question might be too much for him.

"Fine. I'm fine." His voice was shockingly loud in the dim hallway. Mrs. Green had spoken barely above a whisper. And she wore a robe and slippers. *It's the middle of the night,* he remembered, and consciously modulated his volume, though he could feel that weird, toothy smile spreading his face again.

"I'm fine."

Her expression didn't change. "Uh-huh. You know what time it is?"

"Three something?"

"Uh-huh. Close enough. It's *late*. Now, Mr. Green and I have to get up for work in a few hours, and *we* would like to sleep. You think you can keep it down?" She pointed to the front of him. "Maybe clean yourself up a bit?"

He looked down at himself and realized for the first time he was standing here talking to this older woman—he thought she was around his mother's age—wearing only boxer briefs, the front of them still soaked with frozen veggie condensation.

"That's from peas."

"Uh-huh. Well, look, my boy had that same problem, until he was about nine. You can get you some rubber sheets. But clean yourself up, and do it quietly." She pointed the same well-manicured finger back toward her own apartment. "*Mr.* Green said to tell you, you wake him up again, he's gonna come out here and tie your dick in a knot."

Tom was confused by her mention of rubber sheets—his head was a little foggy, and he'd started trembling with the adrenaline still in his system—then realized what it sounded like he'd said. "No—wait, this isn't—"

Tell her about the skeleton monkey, you idiot! Get her husband out here to tie its *dick in a knot!*

"You don't understand!" He threw a thumb over his shoulder toward his apartment door. "There's a—well, it's sort of—"

"*Shhhh!*" Her long finger crossed her lips, and her dark eyes went from cautious to pissed. "Qui-et-ly. You don't want to test Mr. Green's dick tying."

She backed into her apartment, the door closed, and she was gone. Tom stood, thumb over one shoulder, not sure which felt more surreal: that he'd just been chased from his apartment by animate monkey bones, or that his neighbor across the hall, usually quite a sensible woman—at least, according to her—couldn't tell something was seriously wrong here.

"Son of a bitch."

He tried to think what to do. He had the thing trapped, but who was he supposed to call? He still had Officer Bill's card in his wallet, but there was no way that straightlaced guy would—"Oh, wait a minute!" He thunked his forehead with the heel of his hand; his phone was sitting on his nightstand.

Inside the apartment. With the skeleton monkey.

"Shit."

He listened, ear nearly touching the door.

Nothing.

It occurred to him that he'd not heard the thing make a single sound of its own. There had been thumps and bumps, when it struck the door, for example, or the floor, but the thing itself had been perfectly silent. In the movies, a thing like this would have been snarling, spitting, growling, maybe even making that hollow soulless clicking hiss from *Predator*. Christ, that thing had creeped him out as a kid!

But he couldn't hear it in there. Did he dare dash in and try to get his phone? Shit no! And who would he call? He had his keys, so he had his car, but where could he go? Inspiration struck.

"I'll go where that little fucker ain't," he muttered, stepping into his work shorts and yanking them up. His bruised back complained at the quick movements, and his testicle complained loudest of all. "Suck it up, junior," he told it. Both the source of his attack and his strange late-night warning caller were in the same place. "We're off to Wrinkle City."

Chapter 19

Tom gave the door a quick last listen, half expecting to hear the tantruming beastie trashing his place, but there was still nothing. He started down the stairs, the continuing silence nagging at him. Trapped animals freaked out for a while, didn't they? Something about that thought struck him as off, but fuck it, he was no animal expert. He hustled toward the street as fast as his battered body would go, though he did grip the handrail tightly, his recent tumble still fresh in his mind.

He burst though the front door, searching frantically for his car; the old aphorism said, *distance makes the heart grow fonder*, and Tom wanted to be *very* fond of that skeleton monkey.

Dammit! Paul said he left it "on the street out front," but where? I should have looked for it when I got home!

But he'd been sore and tired and just done-in with the long day. Now, at nearly three-thirty am, half naked and crotch damp, he wheeled about on the sidewalk, looking first one way, then the other, then back to the first, muttering, "Fuck-fuck-fuck-fuck—there!"

It was in front of the building next door and across the street. He took a single step toward it, the first move in an intended sprint—when there was a fast *clickety-clickety-click*, a hard impact to his left leg, and then pain like he had never known.

"Fuck!"

He staggered, each movement a tearing pulse of agony, and looked down with a cry. The skeleton monkey had scuttled out of the shadows and flung itself upon his lower leg, wrapping about his shin, the world's ugliest infant taking a footie ride. What had been nagging at him unformed crystalized in an instant: the thing hadn't been trapped—it hadn't gotten *into* the apartment via the door, so who said it needed to get *out* that way?

Its teeth were sunk into his calf right up to its non-existent gums, and the little head jerked sideways, twisting, pinpoints of flame blazing in their sockets. He screamed again.

It's trying to tear that hunk right out of me!

He reached for the thing, terrified, but pain driving him toward a kind of desperate courage; he couldn't flee with it fastened to him, so he'd have to fight. Cold fire burned in the creature's eyes as he shifted weight to that leg, but as Tom touched one cool arm bone, he saw it well for the first time, up close and, unmoving. He froze in a moment of shocked recognition—and it jerked again, and the leg buckled. With a howl, he tumbled backward, the monkey riding his shin like a hideous little bronco buster, clawed finger and toe bones digging in, creating their own sharp points of pain as the jaws worked, biting deeper.

His back hit the sidewalk and he spasmed, bands of pain from the stair bruises locking all his muscles. The horror on his leg took advantage of his momentary paralysis, releasing its bite and scuttling up his body with oily silent speed. Tom felt the pinprick punctures of tiny bones digging in for purchase like a climbing cat rippling up his thigh. It scrabbled over his lap—stomped his abused nut, thank you very much—and then the scratching, stabbing sprint reached his stomach, and he knew where the thing was headed.

Images of Mrs. Nelson's missing face and wide open throat filled his mind, eyeless sockets staring, maggots writing, and he panic-flinched like his mother with a spider, not striking his attacker to hurt or kill it, not even fighting it, really, but flinging his hands up and out with a shriek in a primitive reflex to simply make the bad thing go away. His palms struck bone in a fast, slappy *shove*. There was a sharp tug and a pain in one hand, but the squirming collection of anatomy class castoffs was catapulted through the air. It was light, even for its size, and arced high, arms and legs churning but still eerily silent. Tom had time to roll halfway to his feet—wincing as he put weight on the injured leg, then bellowing when he planted his hands on the cement and something seemed to bite the left one—before it clattered down onto his own front stairs.

Tom lurched to his feet and looked at his hands. The ring finger of the left felt like he'd dipped it in acid, but that wasn't it; the last joint was gone, the tip of the digit neatly nipped off by the skeleton monkey midpush; unaware, he'd just ground the bloody stub into the sidewalk.

"Fuck!"

The front door slammed open and Mr. Green stomped through, barefoot and tying his robe. A warehouse foreman, Tom sometimes wondered if the man had started out *as* a forklift; though nowhere near Dwayne Johnson's stature, Kevin Green was a little larger than average in all directions—a little taller, a little broader, a little thicker—and gave the impression that if anything needed moving, he could move it.

"Goddammit, boy! My Cassie told you—"

There was a sharp *clackety-clack*, a hollow, almost musical sound, like someone rattling small dried bamboo sticks that didn't *quite* make the cut for a wind chime, as the monkey thing righted itself, polished bones gleaming like fresh frost beneath the streetlamp.

"*What* the *fuck* is that," Mr. Green shouted, apparently coming to the conclusion that since *he* was up, the whole neighborhood should be up. He started forward, big bare feet somehow clomping like work boots against the cement stairs. "Is that yours? Well, I'm gonna shove it up your—"

He'd descended two steps when the skeleton monkey whipped around, little feet *tink-tink*ing. The burning eyes must have blazed, for blue-white light flared against Mr. Green's front and face, the man's eyes widening to almost comic roundness.

"*What the fuck is that?*" he shouted again, several octaves higher and even louder than before. He backed toward the door, a mad scrambling parody of his wife in the hall just minutes earlier.

Go ahead, Tom thought. *Show it your dick tying skills*. Rather than answer, Tom took advantage of the creature's distraction to ready his keys and start for his car, limping quickly but quietly, keeping track of the monkey thing over his shoulder. Up and down the street, bedroom lights came on as the thing leapt toward Green, clearing two stairs and landing on the third, covering half the distance between them in a single hop. Green let out a shriek his crew at the warehouse probably never would have believed, unable to take his eyes from the stalking creature, groping frantically behind himself for the doorknob.

"*What the fuck is that?*"

Halfway to his car, Tom hit the lock release, his Toyota letting out a not-very-muted *beep-beep* as the headlights flashed. Halfway up the stairs, the skeleton monkey whirled again, still silent but for the *click* and *rasp* of bones against cement. No longer pinned by the thing's stare, Kevin Green found the knob and disappeared into the building, yanking the door closed hard behind him.

You're welcome! Tom thought, breaking into a lurching run. Eyes front now, determined not to take one of those horror movie slip-trip-and-falls despite his left foot being slick with blood, he heard the thing coming, playing the street like a bamboo drumroll, and just prayed he'd given himself enough of a lead. He hauled the door open and threw himself in, shouting as he swung his legs around and his savaged calf scraped the seat, but never lost focus on that inner doorhandle. He yanked with all he had, determined that if the thing got into the gap he'd smash it to pieces or cut off limbs, but he was closing that god damned door.

The door slammed.

With a rattle and clack, the monkey scrambled over the hood to land on the windshield, little limbs starfished, jaws snapping against the glass. Tom jerked back hard into the seat, but the thing stayed where it was. It tried snapping again, then began raking the glass with its sharp little finger bones, not the frantic, all-out attack it had used on the bedroom door, but with a slow determination, and maybe the thing couldn't chitter or snarl, but those flame-filled sockets *glared.*

Tom took a breath, relaxed a touch, and gave the monkey thing the finger.

"Fuck you, you little monster movie reject."

The monkey didn't scratch any faster, but the softball skull swiveled as the creature inspected the car. Tom's hand shook, and it took him two tries to get the key in the ignition.

"You think you're gonna find a way in here, fucker?"

Cradling his injured hand to his chest, trying not to look down at the mutilated digit, he turned the key. The started whined, then the engine rumbled.

"No chance."

He dropped it into reverse and tapped the gas. The car jerked backward, pulling the hood out from under the skeleton monkey's feet, just as he had the bed sheet, and the thing staggered back from the glass. The Toyota thudded into the car behind it. Tom didn't care, though his heart skipped a beat when the sudden stop threw the monkey back into the windshield.

He dropped the gearshift into drive, cut the wheel hard left, and stomped on the gas. The car leapt out of its spot. The skeleton monkey clung to one windshield wiper as the vehicle careened out onto the street, no longer looking around for a way in; now it stared only at Tom. Snarling, Tom kept his foot on the gas, pushing the car up to thirty, then forty.

"Bu-bye!"

He mashed on the brake. The windshield wiper snapped upright and Mrs. Preobrazhenskaya's skeletal assassin flew through the night clutching a torn-off strip of wiper blade. Tom hoped to see it splash against the tarmac, impact shattering brittle bones like glass, but the creature hit the ground rolling, tumbling two or three yards before somersaulting to its feet. Tom stomped on the gas again even as the thing came to a stop, shouting, "Come on! Come on!"

The Toyota roared up the street, but at the last second the baby-sized bundle of bones flitted out of the way, moving with that sudden, dashing speed he'd seen in the apartment.

"Dammit!"

His blood was up—never mind killing Mrs. Nelson, this little bastard had bitten the tip off his *finger* for fuck's sake—and he hit the brakes again, grabbing the gearshift, fully intending to throw it into reverse and go back for another try, wanting nothing more than to crush this little fucker into dust, then dance on the dust, then maybe *piss* on it—

But there was no sign of the monkey thing in his rearview. If it was off hiding in the shadows, he had no chance of spotting it. *Besides*, he thought, *it's so fucking fast there's no way I'll ever hit it. Confronting Mrs. P's my only chance.* He left the car in drive and accelerated, turning the vehicle toward Fernald Court. Next stop: home of the cookie lady.

Chapter 20

He rolled through the night non-stop, worried the monkey thing might figure out where he was going and try to beat him there. Or maybe Mrs. P. was doing the thinking for it? Was the thing alive? Or was it like some calcareous robot, something to be programmed and turned loose? Or was it more like some black magic marionette, and the old witch was sitting at home pulling its strings? *Was* she a witch?

"Jesus Christ, I don't know *what* the fuck is going on."

The one thing he did know was it all stemmed from the old woman at eighty-two Fernald Court, and he needed to fix this shit now. He took advantage of the middle-of-the-night lack of traffic, speeding along and merely slowing for stop signs and traffic lights. His outer world reduced to a series of street signs and street lights flashing by, while his inner was filled with images of a small skeletal figure dashing tirelessly behind him, arms and legs churning with supernatural speed, pinpoint eye lights bright with anticipation for the kill.

Tom drove faster.

He pulled into Fernald Court and, just as he had hundreds of times over the past year, aimed for the visitor's parking spot. It occurred to him as he killed the engine that he could have just parked right at her building's door. It was more than an hour 'til dawn, and it wasn't like he was there for an actual social call.

"Too late now," he muttered, twisting to pull the door latch with his good right hand then hissing through clenched teeth as he swung his feet out onto the ground;

his calf had stiffened during the drive, settling into a serious but manageable ache, but moving it now sent pain lancing through his leg.

Gotta do this.

Then he was up and limping toward Mrs. P's building, barefoot, battered, and bleeding. He'd grabbed a few fast food napkins from the glove box as he'd driven and wrapped his nubby finger, curling that hand into a fist around the wad to apply some pressure and staunch the bleeding as well as hide it from view; every time he saw the raw meat and protruding bone capping the abbreviated digit, he felt light headed and nauseous. The blood on his calf had cooled and grown tacky, but he was pretty sure it had stopped flowing. He'd not been in a position before to inspect the bite, and chose not to now. He'd get to a hospital later. If there was a later.

He was focused on making it to the cookie lady's door despite his injury, eyes on her building's entryway, but as he passed the Toyota's back bumper, there was a hollow, metallic *tap tap-tap*. He glanced down—and his lurching stride faltered, became a stagger that bit his calf with fresh teeth.

The skeleton monkey clung to his rear license plate, clawed finger bones wedged down between the plate and the car's trunk. It must have dashed out of the way, then leapt back for the car as he passed, grabbing on wherever it could. It had been a twenty minute ride, and Tom had never stopped moving. The creature must have been hanging there the whole time, its weight and the force of every bump and pothole forcing those little bones down farther and farther. Tighter and tighter. The creature struggled to free its left hand. Lacking the weight to bend the plate, it was having to do the whole job through brute strength, but the noise Tom had heard was the creature planting one bony foot above the license plate for leverage. The very edge of the plate was starting to flex.

It took less than a second for Tom to scan for a weapon—a discarded rake in the front flowers perhaps, or a walker left by a front door—and find nothing. It took the rest of the second to realize all he had was a wallet and keys and the shorts covering his ass. The little monster was almost free of the license plate, and he was no longer surrounded by two tons of metal and glass, had nothing but bare skin—skin that had already felt the touch of the creature's claws and fangs—and that crushing, killing rage he'd felt back at his apartment was gone. His only two options were to get back in the car or to run for the old woman's door.

Tom broke into a lumbering, limping sprint. Tears leaked from his eyes as he cursed his wounded leg. The cookie lady's place was two doors down from the visitor's spot, and he wasn't quite halfway there when he heard the nearly musical *tink-tink* of monkey bones dropping to the macadam.

He wasn't going to make it.

"God *damn* it!" *I should have gotten in the car.* He focused on lurching toward Mrs. P's building, but the bamboo drumroll began, and he could hear it catching up fast. The first old folks to rise and shine were going to find him out here, an eyeless, faceless corpse lying in the street wearing nothing but postal shorts and damp undies. He didn't dare look back—still didn't want one of those horror movie falls—but the sounds of the thing had drawn so near they may as well have been xylophone notes played along his own terrified spine. Liquid heat ran down his calf, fresh blood forced from the deep bite as he tried to coax more speed out of that leg. He tried to shout for help, to scream his fool head off, but all that emerged was a high whimper, blubbering sounds in time with his steps. *I should have gotten in the car and driven away, just gotten the fuck out of—*

"In here!"

The front door of the building he was passing swung open, and without a thought Tom veered toward it. The hall was dark, the figure holding the door open just another shadow in the night, but he didn't care; there was a door, a door he could close between himself and the finger-stealing, leg-biting, face-eating thing behind him.

The figure stepped aside and Tom bulled through. His blood-covered left foot met smooth linoleum, found all the traction of a clown stepping on a greased banana peel, and he went down. The impact jarred both calf and finger, and he howled as the door closed behind him. It was a solid outer door, purchased and installed by the housing authority to weather well and last forever. He barely heard the impact the tiny creature made against the metal-wrapped solid core, though the furious scratching came through loud and clear.

"That should hold it awhile. There's no lock, but I don't think it can work the door lever and pull that heavy thing open at the same time. It'll find another way in, though. It always does." The figure—a man, from the voice—shuffled over to the wall.

"Watch your eyes."

The hall lights came on. In the grand scheme of things they weren't very bright—the housing authority wasn't springing for anything more than a sixty-watt bulb for these hallways, no matter *who* lived there—but after running about in the night for so long, Tom found them blinding. He squinted as his savior turned toward him.

"Christ, Tom! You look a mess. Come inside and we can try to keep that murderous little monkey out, and maybe you and me can swap stories."

William Barry leaned down and offered Tom a hand to his feet.

Chapter 21

"What the fuck is going on?"

"In a minute." Mr. Barry helped Tom into his apartment, made sure the door was locked behind them, then led him through the living room into the kitchen and sat him in a wooden chair.

Once seated, Tom asked again, but the old man ignored him, heading off into another room and coming back with a first aid kit the size of a tackle box.

"Got to clean these now. No telling what kind of germs that little bugger's carrying."

He knelt before Tom, showing off the bald spot he normally kept under that fishing hat, and placed the kit on the floor beside him. Tom had been keeping his voice relatively low before, in automatic deference to the hour, but frustration drove him to a near shout. "Wait. Stop, damn it!" Mr. Barry looked up in surprise. Lowering his voice only slightly, Tom asked a third time: "What the fuck is going on?"

"I'm not sure where to begin." The old guy's gaze dropped as he opened the kit. "We might not—"

"Is she a witch?" Tom pointed a trembling finger in the direction of the cookie lady's building. "Is that old grease-faced bitch some kind of witch? Why didn't you ever call back? And it's like four in the morning—how did you know I was coming?"

Mr. Barry lifted a brown bottle from the kit, then a gauze pad in its sterile wrapper. "Keep your voice down. We need to listen. That last is easy: I wasn't sure you were coming, but I knew you were in trouble. I told you that.

I've been listening to the police scanner since back when I was on the paper. It's turned off now, so we can hear if that thing breaks in, but I heard a call earlier about a disturbance at your address—I remember it from when I sent your Christmas card. I still have a good head for things like that: names, numbers, addresses.

"So, I was sitting here feeling bad, because when the phone went I didn't just go straight to someone else's phone. I might have when I was younger, but I'm an old man now. I hesitated—and then it was to late."

"What do you mean, 'too late'?"

"I'll get to that. I should tell what I can in order, or none of this will make sense. So anyway, I'm waiting to hear a body's been found at your place—no offense—but instead they report you left the scene in a white Toyota. So then I'm thinking 'Good, he got away, but where's he gonna go?' and just then I hear a car—you weren't driving subtle—look out the window, and see a white Toyota. You get out, half naked and looking like shit, and start limping for all you're worth. I hurried out to flag you down, and when I opened the door that bone thing was chasing you. And here we are."

While he'd been talking, he'd stripped the wrapper from the gauze and unscrewed the bottle's cap.

"What *is* that thing?" Tom said. "That skeleton thing? It's like ... I don't know. I thought for a while I might have been imagining it, but it scared the shit out of Mr. Green, and I don't figure that guy for being afraid of a lot."

Will Barry shook his head as he measured out a splash of something clear, a quick pour onto the pad. A sharp, medicinal stink touched Tom's nose. "I don't know Mr. Green. And I don't know what that little bone thing is, either." He tilted his head toward the building next door.

"But I know it's real, and I know it comes from *her*. You asked if that old bitch was a witch? Truth is, I don't know." He looked Tom in the eye. "Brace yourself."

"Wha—" Tom began, but the old reporter clapped the hydrogen peroxide-saturated pad to the deep gashes in the back of his calf, and the words turned into a hissing intake of air, then a high, whistling keen as the bubbling, acidic burn set in. Tom thrashed in the chair, legs flailing, but Mr. Barry had been expecting it. He'd knelt close, crowding Tom's feet and angling a shin across his ankles, effectively pinning them.

"Easy! Easy. It'll pass. Give it a minute. So, like I told you before, I don't spy on my neighbors, but that's what Amelia was paying me for. She wanted me to find out how Anna was getting all that stuff out of her apartment. Instead, I found out she was somehow sneaking people *in*."

Tom shook his head and forced words through clenched teeth. "What's all this got to do with that fucking *thing* chasing me? We've got to—"

"I'm getting to that. I was keeping an eye on her windows. Don't judge me, I was being a PI, not a pervert. Anyway, you can't see a lot through those little basement windows in the back, but one night I saw she had company in there. There were two shadows moving round in that back room: hers, which is pretty distinctive, and one tall and thin—definitely not her."

While he talked, the old man swabbed the smaller cuts left by the skeleton thing's fingers.

"I went around the front, trying to see who it was when they left, but no one ever came out. The next morning—I told you I don't sleep much—Anna came out and took the old fogey bus to town. I went and knocked on her door, peeked in her windows. No one had left, but there was nobody in there."

Tom was just getting his breath back, wiping away tears and the sudden rush of snot those tears had released, when Mr. Barry stood, holding out the brown bottle and a fresh gauze packet.

"You want to do your finger, or would you rather I—"

Tom curled his fist tighter about the bloody napkin wad. "You come anywhere near my finger with that shit and *you're* gonna need first aid." He swallowed, took a breath. "So: the skeleton thing?"

Mr. Barry bent to close the kit, then set it on the table. "Mystery packages. Mystery visitor. I put two and two together and started watching her windows after every delivery—whenever she gets one, you leave carrying cookies. And she had them: visitors after each delivery. Different people, sometimes more than one. Doesn't take a genius to figure it out: she gets a package, she gets a visitor, they both disappear. She's dealing in something. But what? Amelia tell you about that one real word? Entrairi?"

Part of Tom was still absorbing that he'd unknowingly been part of a surveillance system, but he nodded. "They thought it was a name, yeah."

"Gave it to a computer researcher I know. He ran with it and came back to me with a warning: leave this shit alone. I had questions, of course. Turns out this Entrairi *is* some sort of name. Comes up in connection with a few things, none of 'em good. Mentioned in the court transcripts after a school shooting back before Columbine. Mentioned by a guy, killed his wife and her whole family Christmas day a few years ago. Stuff like that. Always about buying or selling stuff, always unclear just what was bought or sold.

"That was bad enough, but a couple of his searches led him to the dark web, and that really scared the shit out of him. That's when he quit and gave me the warning."

Even through the pain in his leg, Tom was surprised. "The dark web? That's really a thing? Not just made up for movies?"

"My guy says it's real, and that's good enough for me. He dipped in far enough to find out this Entrairi *is* some kind of seller, but not deep enough to find out what. The word *unnatural* came up a few times, and more than once *supernatural*, and that's all he got before he got out. It was all so weird I never told Amelia about it. I was trying to figure out *what* to tell her when I saw the skeleton thing."

He held up a cautioning hand and cast his gaze around the apartment. Tom did too, noticing for the first time every light he could see was on: ceiling lights, floor lamps, table lamps, everything. The old man focused on Tom again. "Think you can walk a bit?"

"If you're done playing Doctor Mengele on my leg."

"Fine. We need to move around. Look and listen. I said I didn't think that thing could work the door, but that doesn't mean it can't get in here. It has before, and I'm not sure how. If it does again, we need to spot it."

Tom, who'd started struggling to his feet when Mr. Barry said they had to move, sank back down. "What do you mean it's been in here before?"

"Just what I said. Come on. I'll tell you, but we've got to be quiet about it."

Tom managed to stand and shuffled slowly after Mr. Barry, wondering for a moment just who was the old man here. The ex-reporter led him back to the living room, where he opened the front door and peered out into the hall, holding a finger across his lips. After a moment, he closed the door and pulled a pair of canes, one with a pistol grip, the other with the more traditional, crook-style handle, from a doorside umbrella stand. He proffered them both to Tom, eyebrow raised. "You have a preference?"

Tom shrugged, shook his head, and the old man handed him the curl-handled cane, then flipped the other over and held it by the bottom of the shaft, raising it high rather than leaning on it; Tom's was a walking stick, but Will's was a weapon. Creeping across the living room, the old voice was just above a whisper.

"I was watching that back window of hers—she'd gotten a shipment, I was expecting a visitor—but instead of silhouettes against the shade, the shade went up and she opened the window." He moved around the couch with cautious stealth, gaze fixed on the floor lamp in the corner. Tom wondered what the fuck was going on, but then the old guy knelt and leaned down to peer *past* the lamp, into the heating grate set into the wall behind it.

"I was crouching behind the trash cans back there, afraid she'd see me, when this little thing came scuttling around the corner into the alley. It was quick, nothing but a moving shape until it paused on her windowsill. Then I saw the bones."

Holding up a hand, asking for silence, the old man lowered himself to the floor, turning an ear toward the grate and listening for what felt to Tom like forever, but was probably really only twenty seconds. "Thing got in before while all the doors and windows were locked. This is the only way I can think it did it, but if it does now, then we should hear it on the tin. Thing can move fast or quietly, but not both. Have you noticed?"

He rose up to his knees, righted his cane. "I'd just talked to my guy, had the words *unnatural* and *supernatural* in my head, and I may have gasped, I don't know. The little thing whipped around—" Using the cane, he levered himself to his feet with a quiet grunt. "—and I saw two blue-white lights staring right at me before I could duck. I haven't reached the adult diaper stage of being old yet, but I gotta tell you, I nearly pissed my jockeys. Something about the way it moved ..."

Tom remembered the smooth sinuous way the thing had turned to look back at him from Mrs. Nelson's windowsill, the animal quickness it had shown when attacking him, and felt a little tingle along the back of his neck and shoulders. "I've seen it. I get it."

Mr. Barry glanced at him, gaze shooting down to Tom's bloody leg for a moment, showing teeth in a grin that held no hint of humor. "Yeah, I guess you have."

He started for the kitchen, Tom trailing after. "Anyway, past it, in the window, I saw Anna's silhouette, like someone had cut down one of those trees in *The Wizard of Oz* and left just an evil animate stump. The thing went in and the window closed, and I got the hell out of there. Came over here and started calling Amelia—it was the middle of the night, but I didn't care—to tell her I was done, wasn't going to work for her anymore. I didn't know *what* I was going to say about what I'd seen, but I was going to tell her that. Dark web? Bone things that move? I was kind of freaking out."

The old man lowered himself to the kitchen floor, listened to the heating grate, then sat back up to his knees again, planting the cane for the push to his feet.

"She didn't answer. She never answered her phone again." He stood. "I'd talked to her that afternoon, but that was the last I ever saw of her alive. Then you found her yesterday, and it looks like she'd been lying there awhile and ... and I think now what I saw was the thing coming back from killing her, like some kind of hunting dog going back to its kennel."

"Jesus," whispered Tom. "You never went and knocked on her door or anything? Just to see if she was okay?"

The old man looked away. "I ... couldn't. I thought of it, sure, but ... but as far as I know, that *thing* lives over there, or whatever you'd call it, with Anna." He looked back at Tom, and his eyes shone. "I walked by that building every day, and every time I thought about just marching in there, bold as brass, to go up and knock on Amelia's door, maybe go right in if it wasn't locked, like you, but I never did. It seemed too much like just walking into that thing's lair."

He took two steps toward the living room, then stopped, eyes downcast in thought. He swiped at them with the back of one hand.

"Have I mentioned getting old sucks, kid? Besides, the night I saw it, I—"

Thud!

Mr. Barry froze, all round eyes. Tom's own eyes felt huge as he stared back. Holding up a silencing hand again, the old man whispered, barely breathing the words. "Did you hear—"

Click-et-y-click.

Chapter 22

It was quiet, and slow, but it was there—the milky shade of Mr. Barry's face was proof enough to Tom that the old man had heard it too. A stealthy sound, if he'd ever heard one, and it had come from the hall. Or maybe one of the rooms off the hall?

They hadn't heard any glass breaking, or any other kind of noise. "*How'd it get in?*" Tom mouthed.

Mr. Barry shrugged, and his whisper was barely audible. "The night I saw it, I was seriously weirded out. Almost in a panic and not sure what to do. I finally fell asleep for about an hour, and when I woke up, that thing was sitting there on the foot of my bed, watching me with those frigging spooky burning eyes."

"Holy shit!"

"It made sure I saw it, then put a finger across its lips. Teeth. Whatever. It shushed me, then sort of waggled the finger like it was saying *No-no*. It hopped down and left the bedroom, and that was the last I saw of it. You can bet your ass I was done sleeping for the night—the next night, too—but I stayed put until after dawn. Once there was sunlight, I checked the place, but there was no sign of it. It had just been here to deliver a warning: keep quiet and leave things alone."

From down the hall came another quiet *thump*.

"Aw, shit." He was breathing fast, but the old man still raised his cane, half cocked it to swing in the closer confines of the corridor, and started for the hall in a slow creep.

Tom had a thought, a perfectly logical thought that made his stomach sour and bubble while his mouth went powder dry. *All I ever wanted was to just do my job and go* home, he silently objected. Then, with a mental sigh, he slipped his cane up, gripping it from the bottom just as Mr. Barry had, but rather than raise it as a weapon, he reached out to hook the old man's elbow. Mr. Barry whirled, surprised. Tom motioned him closer.

"I'll go first," he whispered.

The old man frowned. "Don't give me any of that *younger man* bullshit." He jerked his chin toward Tom's leg. "You can barely walk on that thing. You can't—"

"I can't get away if it takes you down," Tom whispered. "I'm young and I'm strong, yeah, but I can't run away. *You* can still go for help. Or just get away. Whatever." He felt sick even saying it. Whatever a hero was, he was pretty sure it wasn't someone wearing only postal shorts and armed with a borrowed walking stick.

Mr. Barry's eyes went distant for a moment, considering, then his chin firmed and he nodded.

"My keys are still in the ignition, I think," said Tom, limping forward, still holding the cane like a club. "If it does ... uh ... get me, I'll try to hold it. Slow it down or something. Just ... if you *do* have to run, make it to get help, okay?"

The old man's head pumped. "Yeah. I will, yeah."

Click ... click.

Still quiet, still from the hall somewhere. Still stealthy. Really wishing *he* were the designated *run for help* guy, Tom edged through the doorway. A Persian knockoff runner led the way past three doors: open on the right, open and closed on the left. The ceiling light midway along the short hall was on and bright enough to hurt, the white walls nearly blinding. William Barry seemed to have an aversion to the dark; Tom would have bet it was recently acquired. Cane at the ready, Tom looked back over a shoulder. Pointing and mouthing, Mr. Barry indicated a bedroom on the right, bathroom on the left, and farthest down, the closed door was a closet.

Screw the closet. The thing's not all that deft with doorknobs, so we would have heard something. Tom slipped to the right, into the bedroom doorway. The bathroom would be smaller, and maybe easier to search, but if the thing was looking to hide, it'd have more choices in the bedroom.

Besides, whispered a small, selfish voice from the basement of his brain, *in the movies, the killer's always hiding in the shower, right? So if you're in the bedroom, and the old guy's standing behind you,* between *you and the bathroom* ...

"Shut up," Tom muttered, easing through the open door.

"You see something?" Mr. Barry whispered behind him.

"Just—" Tom reached back, patting the air to shush him. The room was medium-sized and fairly neat, the lack of a second occupant giving it more space; there was just the one bureau, and the bed was a twin bracketed by matching nightstands with matching reading lamps. The narrow closet door hung ajar. Just as in the rest of the place, every light and lamp Tom could see was on, including in that closet.

He glanced over a shoulder, tilting his head toward the half-open door with raised eyebrows.

Mr. Barry shrugged. "Broken latch."

Shit. Tom took a steadying breath—in through nose, out though mouth—hefted the cane in both hands, and limped, as quietly as he could, to the closet. He bent and thumped the door wide with his weapon's rubber foot, then raked the closet floor savagely with the hook, violently stirring several pairs of shoes, one winter boot rolling out to strike his own knee. He straightened as fast as his leg and bruised back would allow, swiping everything hanging from the clothing rod to the right, then left.

Nothing.

He turned to find a wide-eyed Will Barry standing in the middle of the room, his own cane-club raised high, ready to strike. The old man's chest heaved and sweat dappled his forehead like *he'd* been the one flailing through the closet.

Christ, Tom thought. *If the skeleton monkey doesn't get him, a heart attack will.*

He reached out and put a hand on one thin shoulder, giving it a quick squeeze and shake and whispering "Take it easy." The old man jerked his chin in a nod, though his eyes still looked wild as Tom worked his way to his knees to peer under the bed. The spread brushed the carpet. Rather than lift the edge to peek under—how many films had he seen where the investigator wound up with a face full of monster, or with the killer's shiv sicking out of their eye, from pulling just such a maneuver?—he thrust the hook of his cane beneath the bed, hissing explosively with effort and pain as he swept the weapon in a wide arc.

A shape skidded out from under the covers, rolling and tumbling across the rug. With a fierce shout, the pistol grip of Mr. Barry's cane came down like a hammer, smashing the thing once, twice, thrice, each successive blow accompanied by a grunting cry of effort, anger, and fear.

The carpet slipper lay still on the floor, quite dead.

Mr. Barry fell back against the bureau, expression slipping liquidly from aggression through confusion to exhaustion. Hie panted as Tom righted his cane and used it as the old man had after peering into the wall grates, struggled to his feet and stepped close.

"You all right?"

Mr. Barry sucked air. "I … I've made sure to keep all my doors and windows locked since the first time that thing got in. Made sure all the heating grates are on there good and strong. Didn't matter. It got back in earlier tonight. If I'd left as soon as I heard it, or even after I found out the landline was dead, I might have missed it, but the thing was in here. Hiding for a while, then popping up again. Playing with me. I think it cut my phone line, and I know it stole my cell. Then it must have gone off to find you. I can't figure out how it's getting in and out."

He pushed himself away from the bureau, standing shakily on his own two feet.

"I think I got a warning the first time because they'd just killed Amelia. Me dying the same way, just one building over and so soon—I think Anna was afraid it would pull down a serious investigation of the people here, and she definitely doesn't want that. But now you know too, and you're farther away, and she's panicking. I don't know if she's a witch or if that thing out there is just an example of the supernatural whatchamacallits she deals in, but she's like any other dealer in a panic: she means to kill us."

At the mention of supernatural whatchamacallits, Tom remembered his quick flash of recognition while fighting the skeleton monkey, thinking he'd seen that little skull before. He hadn't had time for more than that flash then, and he couldn't quite put his finger on it now.

"Not if we kill her first." That sounded a lot braver than he felt, but, somewhat to his surprise, he found he meant it. He clapped the old guy lightly on the shoulder and limped past him to the hallway—quick look left and right—and across to the bathroom. As Mr. Barry looked on from the doorway, he checked around the toilet and under the sink, then hooked the shower curtain wide, side-stepping with the moving vinyl to avoid the bundle of bones and teeth he imagined leaping for his throat.

Nothing.

"It's here *somewhere*," he whispered to Mr. Barry, who still stood with weapon cocked high, eyes darting here and there.

"I know."

"Where?"

The eyes darted again, and the old man shrugged.

"Come on! This is your place. No ideas?"

"I'm a reporter, not the great white hunter! How the hell should I know?"

A scathing reply rose in Tom, but he pushed it back down, recognizing it as his own fear bubbling up as frustration. The old guy was right, but that didn't stop Tom from wishing he'd just step in with a quick, easy fix, some tidbit of knowledge he'd picked up during his decades working at the paper. It wasn't fair, but fuck fair. What had happened to Mrs. Nelson hadn't been fair. What had happened to him already hadn't been fair. *None* of this was fair, but that didn't mean he had to take it out on Mr. Barry. If not for the old man opening the door for him, Tom would likely have already been cooling meat out in the parking lot, just waiting for early morning discovery.

All that didn't stop Tom from brushing roughly past Will Barry and limping back down the hall. Following, Mr. Barry said, "It's my place, yeah, but I can't even figure out for sure how the little bastard's getting in."

Tom got as far as the end of the hall, where it opened out into the living room, and lurched to a halt. "Shit. I think I can help you there." He pointed up over the couch, where one of the acoustical ceiling tiles sat cockeyed to the rest, pulled out of the frame and resting atop it rather than seated in it, leaving a gap, a hole up into the dark airspace above. Behind him, Mr. Barry whispered, "Shhhhhit."

In a flash, Tom understood how the old man had missed it. Those tiles couldn't support more than a few pounds without cracking, and even the framework of struts wasn't designed to hold up much more than the tiles themselves. No normal creeper could have done it without breaking through, but the skeleton monkey, so small and lacking even the meager weight of any meat on its bones, could have scampered across it like a hardwood floor. There was even a layer of fiberglass insulation atop the tiles, Tom saw, thin, but enough to deaden noise between apartments; probably enough to allow the little thing to move about quite silently.

It'd go right over the tops of these walls up there, he thought, *and those little fingerbones might not be able to work a doorknob well, but they'd be fucking awesome at prying up those tiles. Shit, the little fucker could be anywhere—even back where we just looked for it.*

He turned to whisper that maybe they should just get the hell out of there, retreat to his own apartment, where he didn't have dropped ceilings, to regroup and come up with a plan—and shouted instead.

"Look out!"

The skeleton monkey was knuckling up the hallway behind the old man at full speed.

Chapter 23

The long runner deadened the *clickety-click* of its pounding claws, helping the thing maintain its eerie silence. Bones gleaming in ceiling fixture brilliance, light glinting off the fangs jutting from its wide open mouth, the thing leaped, arms spread, just as Mr. Barry wheeled. The old man was still raising the cane to defend himself when the silent horror struck him full in the face.

With a shriek, Mr. Barry swung, but whether he was actually trying to bat the thing from him or it was just a reflex move, Tom couldn't tell. Halfway through the swing, the old hands snapped open, and the cane flew down the hall. Mr. Barry grabbed and slapped at the thing, trying to push it away, but the skeleton monkey had its talons in, hugging the old man's head just as it had wrapped itself around Tom's leg in the street. Tom started forward—raising his own cane, though he had no idea how he'd hit the thing without smashing his friend's head—but Mr. Barry fell back. Tom tried to get out of the way, but his left leg wasn't up to the fast change of direction. The back of the thin old shoulders slammed into his shins and he sprawled backward as well. His ass landed on the sofa armrest and he flipped over it. He came down only half on the cushions, rolled left, and sprawled facedown on the rug in front of the sofa, Will Barry's screams ringing in his ears.

"Help! Help me! Help *meeeeeeeee*!"

Words rose into a long, steam whistle shriek.

Tom got his hands under him, shoved and twisted and sat up, trying to leave his left leg out of the maneuver. Mr. Barry lay on his back just beyond Tom's feet, one hand flailing, the other somehow wormed up between him and his attacker, planted against the smooth white breastbone, pushing weakly but without success. The creature remained locked on with a four-footed grip as that steam whistle sound went on and on. Tom couldn't see Mr. Barry's face, but there was blood splashing the shiny skull atop him—and then the thing rose up to look at Tom.

Mr. Barry's eye hung from one of the grotesque canines, pierced and scooped out like an oyster from its shell, red stringers of tendon stretching down to the socket Tom couldn't see. The sockets of the monkey skull stared right at him though, and deep within them, visible again now that the thing was out of the over-bright hallway, those blue-white lights gleamed like gas flames, and though the bony skull was incapable of expression, those flames looked somehow pleased.

As those red strings tensed and pulled, the steam whistle scream rose and the old man pushed harder, lifting the rising creature higher. In horrified desperation, perhaps recalling the success of the thawing bag of peas, Tom snatched a cushion from the couch and fired it at the thing's gore-covered grin as hard as he could. It was heavier than the peas, and more awkward to throw, but the leading edge caught the top of Will Barry's head and spun the five pound cushion right into the skinless simian face.

The shriek cut off at the seat cushion's impact, and Tom heard a *snap* as the skeleton thing tumbled away. Tom rolled, flopping onto his face again, shoving himself to his feet, forcing his leg to comply though he felt the gashes in his calf tearing wider. The scream started again, this time deeper, more guttural, and the old man seemed to be trying for words. Weight on his right leg, using his left mainly for balance, Tom spun awkwardly to face the skeleton monkey, looked down—and straight into Mr. Barry's remaining eye.

The old man had struggled over onto his stomach as well, but couldn't seem to make it to his feet. He clawed his way forward in a clumsy army crawl, and in his mind, Tom saw Mrs. Nelson, faceless and bloated, swimming toward the door, in almost the exact position and place Will Barry was now. Some of those red strings that had formed her peek-a-boo cheek hung from his raw socket. The eye was gone, and flaps of bloody flesh dangled from his face beneath each ear, where the creature's fishhook fingers had been ripped free, skinning back layers of flesh and muscle as easy as peeling an orange.

"Tom ... help me ..."

This isn't how it was supposed to work! Tom thought, even as he started forward. *He was going to run for help! I should be running now, while he holds it off—bad luck for him, but for me ...*

But he couldn't do that, even though part of him wanted only to run right out of there, to say fuck the old man, fuck the leg, fuck the old lady—shit, to say fuck everything about this place, to just get in the Toyota and drive west until his debit card couldn't get him any more gas or he hit the Pacific, whichever came first. Mr. Barry was one of his friendlier customers, someone he looked forward to talking to, despite the man's tendency to just bang on and on. Dude could tell a story. And now the fear, the absolute terror in that one brown eye ... He'd opened the door. He'd let Tom in. Tom couldn't leave.

Tom bent, one hand locked on the cane, now righted and holding him up again, and reached down to haul the old guy to his feet. There was nothing wrong with those old legs, was there? Tom was the one with the limp, and he was ready to run. "The hospital," he said as thin trembling fingers took his hand in a death grip and he started to pull. "My car. We've got to go before that thing comes—"

There was a rapid *clickclick*, bone on hardwood as the thing crossed the gap between the hallway runner and the living room rug. Every light in the place burning, there were no shadows for the monkey to pounce from, but it didn't need them. The thing ran up Will Barry's back, all four limbs scrabbling with that darting animal quickness, jaws set wide to attack, the old man's missing eyeball still hanging from one two-inch fang, hellish sockets *burning*, so fast Tom barely had time to register it was coming before it was there. The *Look out!* hadn't yet reached his mouth before the small smooth skull twisted sideways, like that old RCA dog, the bloody bone claws wrapped themselves in the old man's collar, and the thing snapped forward like a striking snake, burying its teeth in the side of the wrinkled old neck.

The warning turned into a wordless yell as the skull jerked sideways, the whole little body reared back hard, and the skeleton monkey tore out the side of the old man's throat. The hand gripping Tom's spasmed, squeezed hard enough to make Tom cry out. Hot blood sprayed over him from just two feet away, systolic pressure causing the stuff to burst from the wound even as Will Barry's toes beat a panicked tattoo on the rug—Tom had a quick flash of little kids kick-kick-kicking as they learned to swim, then old Mrs. Nelson, freestyling toward the door, face split in an inhuman grin—and the old man's attempted scream puffed his atomized life out onto the rug. The stuff covered Tom's chest and face, got in his mouth, and half blinded him, but Mr. Barry's own visage remained strangely untouched; Tom had a clear view of that terror fading from the man's single eye as the kicking feet slowed, the light in it winking out as the iron grip went slack.

And the skeleton monkey turned to look at him.

"No-no-no—" He dropped the loose hand as the thing perched on the dead man's back opened and closed its jaws, dropping the gobbet of flesh that had so recently held Mr. Barry's life inside his skin. It shook its head, trying to loose the crushed remains of that single eyeball, still impaled on a long curved canine but now mashed up into the other teeth like a squashed grape; red streamers of tissue dangled from it, swinging out left and right like runners of drool that just wouldn't break.

"Fucking thing!"

Tom didn't bother reversing the cane the way he had before, he just swung as fast and hard as he could. The monkey thing ducked back—it wasn't like a movie zombie, it had *some* sense of self-preservation—and Tom nearly fell when his stupid leg threatened to fold over the torque. He hopped forward, bringing the cane up and down, the thin wood moving through the air so fast it hummed, but the beast wasn't there when it arrived. Mr. Barry's body jumped at the impact.

So what? Tom thought, hop-shuffling a little sideways for balance. *He can't feel it! He's dead! The old man is dead, and I'm going to wind up the same, I'm going to wind up the same, I'm going to wind up—*

He recognized his hysteria just as he had back in his own front hall, but this time there would be no Cassandra Green to help him snap out of it. He was on his own, squared off with the monkey thing: he with a cane held before him in a shitty facsimile of a samurai with his sword, the product of countless hours spent watching Asian cinema rather than any actual training; it running back and forth, left and right, like an agitated zoo animal rapid-pacing the cage bars though there were no bars between them, just the prone body of one old man. Tom suppressed a giggle. Even in his hysteria, he recognized the disadvantage he was at here. He had the cane, sure, but the thing had speed, mobility, and an obvious ability to kill. Even Mr. Barry's body was an advantage to the creature: it was a barrier to Tom, who, with his fucked up leg, couldn't confidently leap or even just step over, but to the skeleton monkey it was nothing. It might even be used as a springboard, allowing the hateful horror to leap higher and farther.

It knew it, too; Tom could tell from the way it danced about just out of reach, goading him to take a swing, maybe stumble over his friend's corpse and fall on his face. That would remove the cane as a threat as well as drop his head and throat right down into the creature's strike zone. The urge to catch up with the thing, to swing and swing until the old woman's monster was nothing but a pile of shattered shards, was huge. But chasing it seemed to be what it wanted, and would likely be playing right into its blood-covered little claws. He swiped the cane in another short arc, not chasing but threatening, and wondered again, in a flash, whether the thing was some version of alive or if it were merely a kind of puppet, whether the old woman simply wound it up and let it go, or if she was over there right now tranced out, controlling her weapon like a kid at the park flying an RC drone. Could she see him? Hear him?

"Fuck you, you old cunt."

Just saying the words helped him focus, a little anger mixing with the terror that had loomed so large and blocked out everything else. He expressed the sentiment again and again, using it as a mantra, pushing down his fight-or-flight-reflex and letting him *think*. "Fuck you ... fuck you ... fuck you ..." he muttered, backing toward the kitchen. It was all he could do to take control of the situation: get the thing to follow him, rather than the other way around. He had the cane up over one shoulder now, more like a bat than a sword. The thing had leapt at him in his apartment, and it had leapt at Mr. Barry.

Jump at me now, he thought. *I'll grand slam you right through the fucking wall.*

When he started backing away, the bone thing stopped running back and forth and stood square on with him, rocking rapidly from side to side, agitated, still moving in that simian way that had helped Tom identify it from a single glance back in Mrs. Nelson's apartment. As he reached the threshold between rooms, wishing heartily the place had been built with a kitchen door rather than an open arch, the creature hunched, spreading arms and jaws wide. If it had still possessed a larynx, Tom imagined it would be screaming a challenge right about then.

Come on! Come on! he thought, but his mouth seemed stuck on his mantra, the mutter rising to a shout. "Fuck you! Fuck you!"

Self-confidence was good; it kept him moving. But he'd never played on a team, and had only messed around at the batting cages, and the odds of him actually hitting a flying attacker were less than stellar. As long as he kept his feet, though, he had a chance, no matter that his leg was screaming at him. The hurt was good. The hurt meant he was alive. Right here and now, if the hurt stopped—he thought of the terror fading from Mr. Barry's eyes as the man's life erupted from his torn throat, and glanced down at the body lying at the skeleton monkey's feet—it meant he was dead.

Fuck that.

He'd been in these units before—Mrs. Nelson had said they all had the same floor plan—helping with water bottles and wine, but he hadn't been looking for an escape route then. *But these ground floor units, they have to have some kind of back door, don't they? And that would lead out from the kitchen, wouldn't it?* And with that thought, that escape might be just behind him, Tom couldn't help but glance back to see if he was right.

And in that moment of distraction, the skeleton monkey struck.

Chapter 24

As he crossed into the kitchen, Tom snuck a peek over one shoulder, searching for the door he hoped was there—and looked back to see the monkey in midair, sailing toward him, arms and jaws spread. He swung, trying to hit the promised home run, but even though he'd been looking for it, its eerie silent quickness had caught him off-guard. His footing was wrong, his swing slow, and something—fang or talon, he didn't see which—scored on his left wrist as the thing flew past. The cane went flying as the monster landed on the table behind him. He turned, twisting to keep his attacker in view, not wanting to give the creature his back, as the old man had, but the thing caught the table's edge with one handlike foot and reversed direction instantly, leaping at him again.

Tom flung his arms up before his face, trying to catch the little monster as he had in the street in front of his building, send it flying again, but the monkey thing had anticipated the move and came in low. It slipped by him once more, passing Tom's legs in midair, and pain exploded from the back of his right knee, slashed with tooth or claw. His right leg buckled, his left wasn't a lot of help, and, twisting as he was, Tom went sprawling. His ribs slammed into the counter edge and fresh agony bloomed as he felt something crack. His right arm swung, groping for anything to stop his fall, but all he managed was to sweep the counter clean, scooping an avalanche of kitchen junk down with him.

He landed facedown amid a scattering of recipe books and a tumbled bowl of apples, clutching a Magic Bullet juicer in one hand, and there was pain. Pain from his freshly cut leg keeping him from getting up, pain from his ribs keeping him from breathing. He was on the floor right where he hadn't wanted to be, and the skeleton monkey was coming. Coming from behind, just as it had Mrs. Nelson. Just as it had Mr. Barry. There was nothing he could do about it. He lifted his gaze from the linoleum before him, wanting to find that back door he knew must be there, to see how close he'd come before falling. Failing.

And right in front of him lay another thing his flailing arm had swept from the counter: the heavy wooden block holding Mr. Barry's nice sharp knives.

It lay on its side, most of the smaller knives spilled and scattered, but the bigger, longer blades had hung up in the block.

From behind came a quick *clackety-clack*, the transition from living room rug to kitchen linoleum heralding the entrance of the skeleton monkey moving at a run. Tom flailed at the knife block as the quick sound stopped.

It's leaping!

He grasped a handle, blindly jerked it free, and pushed with his left hand and foot, screaming with the pain coming from that leg. It wasn't pretty, but he managed a quick flop, a hobnailed bootheel of pain grinding into his side as things in there that shouldn't move moved, thrusting up at the shape falling toward him—a shape that was in midair and couldn't change direction.

The way things had been going, Tom might have expected that he'd snagged the paring knife—the only one in the block smaller than those scattered steak knives—but luck finally fell in his favor, and the broad-bladed butcher's knife shot up to meet the attacking bones. He saw the creature coming almost in slow-motion, small but growing as it drew nearer, arms and jaws wide, as he knew it would be. Its head started the sideways twist that would allow it to slip in under Tom's chin—the better to tear out your throat, my dear—and then that head jerked to a halt, a small hairless dog run out to the end of its chain. The body snapped downward, rear claws even kicking out but falling short in an effort to reach the target, before all four limbs wrapped around Tom's arm, a fireman trapped midway down the pole, everything held in place by the shiny knife blade thrusting up between the fangs to impale the roof of the skeleton monkey's mouth.

Tom's triumphant shout turned into a wordless cry as all four feet raked his bare arm, clawing deep and drawing blood. The blue-white flames in those sockets blazed as the bone creature struggled, stuck but by no means finished. Tom, on the other hand, knew he was done. Neither leg would be all that useful if he had to flee, and the thing was rapidly shredding his right arm. If he let go the knife, the thing would be free in an instant and barely the worse for wear. He was running out of time, and did the only thing that came to mind: he let himself fall back and rolled, smashing the knife with all his waning strength into the cabinet door beside him, then let it go and rolled away.

The tip of the blade had pierced the top of the skull—barely—and the skeleton thing hung squirming from the blade nailing it to the walnut-stained door. Tom started to turn away, wanting only to go, to crawl if he had to, but to leave the thing for someone else to find, for someone else to finish. But even as he did, small skeletal hands reached up to grip the blade while tiny bone legs kicked, throwing what little weight the creature had into the effort. Head bent back at an unnatural angle, skull pierced in a fashion that would have killed anything living—and *should* have put down anything undead, according to the movies—the deadlights in its sockets burned as brightly as ever as the thing worked to free itself, the handle of the knife already wiggling as the door's grip on the blade tip loosened.

Tears leaked from Tom's eyes as he shouted "Why won't you die? Why won't you fucking die?"

The creature's only answer was a silent blazing stare from the one eye aimed in Tom's direction, and the handle wiggled a wider arc.

Tom fell back on his previous mantra.

"Fuck you."

He leaned over and scooped the wooden knife block close.

"Fuck you."

Nubby finger complaining shrilly, he gripped it clumsily in both hands. The blood in his palms made it slick but he managed to pull it to his chest, left arm having to do most of the work as something in his bleeding right forearm failed to function.

"Fuck you!"

He thrust the block against the butt of the wiggling handle, an awkward but heavy hammer. Something ground and tore in his side, stealing his breath in an agonized whistle, but with a hollow *boom* from the cabinet, the sharp blade drove deep into the door. With the short wet *prrip* of a knife sectioning a nice ripe apple, the little skull split neatly in two, bifurcated right between the sockets. The gas flame eyes flared and winked out, and even as the twin halves of skull fell away from the pinning blade, the rest of the skeleton came apart, raining down on the floor like a hideous game of pick-up-sticks.

Tom sat on the floor, catching his breath and clinging to the world. The world tried to go away, went a little wavery and gray for a bit, but he repeated his mantra and held on to one thought with everything he had: *It's not over.*

Of course it wasn't over. The skeleton monkey, as terrible as it had been, had only been an errand boy. A tool. He'd gotten in his car earlier—what, had that just been this evening?—intending to confront the cookie lady, to try to get her to stop whatever it was she was doing. To get her to leave him alone.

Still got to talk to her, he thought, dragging himself across the floor with his left arm and leg—something behind his right leg had been severed, promoting his left leg to *good leg* status—to his dropped cane. *Even if I'm not laid up in the hospital, and Christ, I hope I'm laid up in the hospital*—He struggled to his feet using a combination of cane and counter—*I'll be in no shape to do fuck all if she sends another thing after me.*

Because he had no idea if she would. If she *could.*

But she's a hundred and nine. At least. He took an experimental swing with the cane. He wasn't all that steady, and there wouldn't be any dancing around with it, and he really only had his clumsy left arm to work with, but still. *She's got eighty years on me. If I can't convince her with this …*

Blue and red lights flashed in the front room. Someone else in the building had heard the all the commotion and called the police. But this was old age housing, and they got called out here fairly often, usually because someone had found a body or fallen and couldn't get up. There wasn't any noise now, and Tom figured they'd waste a little time knocking on the door asking to be let in, looking for a response before forcing the lock. He caned his way slowly to the other side of the kitchen.

"Oh look, I was right. A back door."

He slipped quietly out into the pre-dawn darkness. Limped up the alley between buildings to the front, where he found a single police car, roof lights whirling and flashing. Both officers seemed to be in the hall at Mr. Barry's door, so Tom made his unhurried way around to the front of 81–84 Fernald Court.

"Tom?"

The voice was old and quavering, and Tom didn't recognize it, but it had to be one of the residents, come out to see what all the fuss was about. He didn't turn. Didn't pause. Just opened the door and entered the building.

It was only four steps down to the lower hall and the cookie lady's door, but they almost defeated him. He stumbled, and if he'd fallen it would have been the end of him; there was no way he would have gotten up. But he caught himself with the sturdy, built-for-the-elderly handrail, and made the last step.

He didn't knock. Her door was unlocked. He opened it and staggered in.

"Mrs. Preobrazhenskaya?" He wheezed in a breath. A dagger of pain wiggled in his side, "You cunt. You in here?"

He limped slowly through the her living room, made his way around her coffee table—no little skull under the remote any more, he noticed—toward the bedroom. He knew where it was now; Mrs. Nelson had said the units were all the same. Unlike Mr. Barry's hall, this one was dark, though a soft, yellow, old-bulb light spilled from the open bedroom door.

"I've come to kill you. But you know that, right?"

He wheezed. Limped to the open doorway. Stopped.

Mrs. Preobrazhenskaya lay on the bed in her horrid yellow housecoat, one bare and callused foot hanging out in space, face covered with clear goop, eyes open but unseeing. Her left eye, the one toward him, was bloodshot, bugging from her head in cartoonish surprise, while something dark stained the pillow beneath her left ear. Her impressive bosom neither rose nor fell, but lay as still as that pile of bones in Mr. Barry's kitchen; as still as William Barry himself.

A small sound rose up from Tom's chest—small, but happy, until the pain cut it short. Almost a chuckle.

"Huh-huh. Ding-dong, looks like the witch is dead."

That's when one of the cops tackled him from behind shouting, "Drop the stick! Drop the stick!" The world finally got its wish, and slipped away.

Rob Smales

Chapter 25

He'd hoped everything would be cleared up by the time he got out of the hospital, but it took a little longer than that.

He was officially charged with the murder of William Edwin Barry, but the charges were dropped quickly. Well, *relatively* quickly. When Tom's lawyer pointed out in chambers that: the ME said Will Barry'd died from an animal attack; Tom had a similar wound on the back of one calf; whatever struggle *had* gone on in that apartment—everyone attributed Tom's tale of a skeleton monkey to shock, or hysteria, or simply *that guy's fucking nuts*—had continued, according to the way the blood patterns in the apartment overlayed each other, *after* William Barry was dead; and that Thomas Daniel Galvin had suffered *more* injuries than the victim, many of them nearly as grievous, and several of them *after* the fatal wounding of William Barry (forensics experts chimed in at several points), the prosecutor had thrown up his hands and dropped the charges. In the only interview he gave (to *The Globe*, Mr. Barry's old outfit), Tom thanked his lawyer—a public defender he'd been assigned, he wasn't made of money—and the police for their diligent investigation of the crime. They'd been pushing hard trying to put together a slam-dunk case against him, of course, but so much of what had gone into the official reports had been in Tom's favor, he figured, what the hell? They deserved an *attaboy*.

He was never charged with anything in relation to the death of Ms. Anna Preobrazhenskaya. Though found in her bedroom armed with a cane, there was no external evidence of violence on the body, and he'd been seen entering her building barely a minute before police caught up with him. Tom claimed not to remember why he'd gone in there, or even that he *had* gone in there, and when his attending physician—much to the annoyance of the questioning cops—had floated the idea of confusion due to shock, Tom grabbed onto that phrase and never let go. The official cause of death was a ruptured brain aneurysm, and there was no way he'd caused *that*, was there? Though Tom *did* harbor thoughts about cutting the mental strings on a magical marionette being debilitating for both the puppet and puppeteer, he kept them to himself.

There was no mention in any report of finding any bones, simian or otherwise, in Mr. Barry's apartment, though the papers and TV news ran a nice glossy eight-by-ten shot of the butcher's knife sticking out of that cabinet door. Nor did there appear to be a huge stockpile of items, antique or otherwise, with Anna Preobrazhenskaya's name on it. Everything in her apartment was perfectly mundane and normal, at least as far as anyone could tell.

Tom was done as a letter carrier. Surgeons did what they could to repair the damage to his right lateral hamstring tendons, but even after the long hours of physical therapy in his future, there was a good chance he'd always walk with a limp. Paul was seeing what he could do to transfer Tom over to the clerk's side of things, where an inability to walk long distances wouldn't matter as much. They did a lot of it over the phone, while Tom lay in a hospital bed (interspersed with Paul's questions about just what had gone on in that apartment, though, he reported with glee, the skeleton monkey story was just *killing* Neery), but eventually, once he was up and about a little—and the whole court drama had ended—Tom decided to go in to the office to talk to Paul face-to-face. He'd been kind of lonely in the hospital, and now, recuperating in his apartment, and it'd be good to see some of the people he'd worked with for years. Besides, it might help him decide whether to stay at the post office or not. Paul was being *really* helpful, but Tom was still kind of on the fence about it.

He crutched his way through the swinging doors from the rear parking lot onto the workroom floor, and Paul was up out of his seat in an instant, arms spread in welcome.

"Dude! Good to see you getting out and around! Miss the place that much, huh? It's me, right? You don't have to say it. I'll give you a picture to take home so you can pine for me in private. How about a selfie with me? Want to take a selfie?"

Tom laughed. "Sure. I'd like nothing better." He swung a crutch toward the chair Paul had just vacated. "I know it's your desk and all, but mind if I sit down?"

"Sure, park your ass. I got some stuff for you anyway."

Tom lowered himself into Paul's butt groove and raised an eyebrow. "Stuff?"

"From your customers. Mostly out at Fernald Court." Paul reached behind his desk and pulled out a shoe box filled with envelopes of various colors and sizes, most with Tom's name on them, though some simply said some version of *To My Postman*. "Sue's been covering your route for the most part, and your folks have been leaving these out for you. She was keeping them in your drawer for a while, but more came the longer you were out, and they started to get in the way, so I put 'em here."

Of course, Tom thought, and felt his eyes go wet—though he'd be damned if he'd shed an actual tear in front of Paul.

He'd never hear the end of it. *Without Mr. Barry to track down my address, they had nowhere else to send them.*

"There's one other thing. I'll be right back."

Paul strode off, leaving Tom opening envelopes and reading get well cards. He wasn't shocked to have a few—some customers did that kind of thing, around Christmas for example—but he *was* surprised at how *many*. It was like they'd clubbed together to make sure everyone at Fernald Court had wished him well.

Or, maybe, they'd all *known something was hinky about the cookie lady. Mr. Barry really was* terrible *at keeping his mouth shut. Could he have let something slip?* He thought of the space the crowd had left around Mrs. Preobrazhenskaya the day he'd found Mrs. Nelson. *Could they all have been, if not afraid of the woman outright, at least a little unnerved by her? Do they all think, maybe, I had a little something to do with her death after all, and they're ... thankful?*

He planned to never, ever set foot in Fernald Court again—to avoid that whole section of town, if possible—so he'd likely never know. He could live with that.

"Had to get this from the registry." Tom looked up to see Paul thump something down on the desk in front of him with a grin. "You'll have to sign for it, of course."

It was a package the size of another shoe box, wrapped in brown paper and covered with more international post stamps than Tom thought there were countries. The shipping label on top was filled out entirely in what Tom now knew only *looked* like the Cyrillic alphabet, except for ... yes, he searched for it and found a single word: *ЕНТРАРИ.*

"*Entrairi,*" he whispered.

"Your very own fourteen-inch solid rubber dildo," Paul announced, voice dripping with joy. Tom tore his gaze from the faux Cyrillic lettering and looked at the destination field: Thomas Galvin, care of the post office.

Holy shit! It is *for me!*

There was a *snick*, and Paul's hands poked into his field of vision, one bearing the pen and slip for him to sign, the other an open pocket knife.

"Go on. Sign for it and open it up."

Tom blinked up at his supervisor. "What, right here?"

Paul bounced both hands. "Dude. I been staring at that box over in the registry for two weeks. If you don't open your dildo right here and now, so I can see, I'm gonna cry myself to sleep every night for a fucking year. Please."

Tom scrabbled about in his brain for some graceful way to say no, but came up empty. He signed the slip and accepted the pocket knife, pushing himself up to his feet to slice the packing tape. Flipping the top flaps back revealed a square of soft foam rubber padding. Tom lifted the padding—and fell back into his chair, eyes wide.

"*Holy shit*," Paul whispered. "That's ... I ..." He spun away and strode off for another part of the post office. "Neery! You *got* to see this! You'll puke!"

Nestled down into their own layer of foam rubber lay two halves of a small skull, split neatly down the middle, polished bone gleaming in the overhead fluorescents, fangs and teeth white enough to star in a Crest commercial and showing no hint of blood. Below the cloven monkey skull lay a folded sheet of paper. With trembling fingers, Tom plucked up the paper and smoothed it open.

Bill of Sale was printed across the top. Beneath it was a note written with black ink in a fine, flowing hand: *You break it, you bought it.*

One of the lines set out for itemizing the purchases was filled with more of those strange, non-Cyrillic symbols, but beneath it was another hand scrawl in English: *Paid in full.* In the box headed *Paid By* was a typed name: Anna Preobrazhenskaya.

At the very bottom of the sheet was the last of the black ink handwriting.

Pleasure doing business with you.
—Entrairi

We hope that you enjoyed this title and look forward to many more to come. Please, leave us a review! Reviews matter to all of our authors.

Take a look at some of our other award-winning series at https://threeravenspublishing.com/series-universes/

Visit us at https://www.threeravenspublishing.com and sign up for our newsletter for the latest and greatest news on upcoming titles and events.

Other series and titles you might enjoy.

BIOLOGIC   ENHANCED   NASCENT   TALENT

IT CAME FROM THE
TRAILER PARK

You can also keep up to date with our latest release announcements on Scifi.radio and get some of the best fandom programing on the planet.

Scifi for your Wifi

And don't forget to check out our other Sponsors and Affiliates

A southern Appalachian jewel for craft beer lovers, Buck Bald Brewing offers something for everyone.

To discover more visit us at buckbaldbrewing.com

Revolution X is a testament to the power of collaboration, blending four unique styles into a cohesive, revolutionary sound. When these four individuals unite, the result is nothing short of musical Revolution!

Would you like to learn how to write and market your own titles? The following affiliates links might be helpful.

Don't forget to check out the latest edition of Car Warriors: Autoduel Chronicle fiction series.

https://threeravenspublishing.com/car-warriors-autoduel-chronicles/

...or the latest in the *Car Wars* game series

http://www.sjgames.com/car-wars/

Or the other amazing titles from
Steve Jackson Games

STEVE
JACKSON
GAMES

http://www.sjgames.com

Comprised of active or retired servicemen and civilian volunteers, Shepherd's Men enthusiastically raises awareness and funds for the SHARE Military Initiative (SHARE) at Shepherd Center in Atlanta, GA.

This nationally renowned program focuses on assessment and treatment for American military veterans who have sustained mild to moderate Traumatic Brain Injury (TBI) and Post-Traumatic Stress Disorder (PTSD) during post-9/11 service.

Find out more at: https://www.shepherdsmen.com/

Milton Keynes UK
Ingram Content Group UK Ltd.
UKHW040254291024
450401UK00005B/13